TEMPLAR HERESY

"An erudite, gripping novel of one man's journey, set during the tumultuous Crusades, where a series of totally unexpected twists and turns leads to a subsequent initiation process, creating extraordinary transformative changes, forever altering his perception of himself, the world, and those around him. This fascinating account parallels a far greater universal theme—that of a profound spiritual quest of heart and soul, of timeless wisdom and raw courage, where definitions and boundaries change, new doorways open as others close, where peace is valued and challenges are met, and longstanding cultural 'mythconceptions' on both sides undergo a dramatic metamorphosis—never to be the same again! A riveting read, the kind you can't put down . . . a panacea for a battle weary world."

KAREN RALLS, PH.D., MEDIEVAL HISTORIAN,
WORLD RELIGIONS AND SPIRITUALITY SCHOLAR, AND AUTHOR OF
The Templars and the Grail, Gothic Cathedrals,
AND *Knights Templar Encyclopedia*

"James Wasserman has risen to the challenge of the daunting task of making medieval history, and especially esoteric history, entertaining and compelling. Things were so very different then, but some things never change. Wasserman has located the spiritual Gnosis in relations between a few remarkable Templars and the survivals of the antique Gnosis in Syria and Languedoc. *Templar Heresy* is a story of personal illumination the reader can easily share because it is clearly, sincerely, and excitingly expressed."

TOBIAS CHURTON,
AUTHOR OF *The Invisible History of the Rosicrucians*

"*Templar Heresy* is a unique tale of spiritual growth and initiation— words that have been so abused of late they seemingly have little meaning. In his rescuing of these sacred terms, Wasserman creates a teaching tool of vital importance. Unlike similar books, loosely wrapped in a historical veneer or vague spiritual teachings (often channeled from a past life), *Templar Heresy* is rigorous in its spiritual content and historical context. Readers cannot come away unchanged—as *Templar Heresy* will teach you about the past, the present (and possibly give a glimpse of the future), as well as authentic spiritual initiation. It will also teach you something about yourself. Readers be warned!"

MARK STAVISH, DIRECTOR OF STUDIES
FOR THE INSTITUTE FOR HERMETIC STUDIES

"Historians struggle to strip away the dark veils of the ancient days and reveal just a glimpse of the panorama of life in the distant past. The attempts are frequently pallid portraits of times that cry out for a rich palette of many tones with the deft hand of an artist. In *Templar Heresy*, James Wasserman gives us just such a vivid portrait of the burgeoning disparate movements of the medieval Crusades—from the infamous cult of Assassins to the Order of the Knights Templar. The evolution of the Western esoteric tradition is revealed as we follow the lives of Sinan the Assassin and the Templar Roland de Provence through these journeys of Spiritual Aspiration and Realization, Betrayal and Persecution, Love and Reconciliation. This is history imbued with the colors of life that only life can reveal. *Templar Heresy* is a dramatic tour de force not to be missed."

J. DANIEL GUNTHER,
AUTHOR OF *Initiation in the Aeon of the Child*

"Wasserman's style is delightful. He reminds me of classical French authors like Alexandre Dumas the younger. Moving straight ahead with his story, he wastes no time with excessive explanation while providing a real study of the political circumstances of the period. This book brings together accurate and insightful historical investigation with well-written and intuitive storytelling."

GEORG DEHN,
EDITOR OF *The Book of Abramelin: A New Translation*

TEMPLAR HERESY

A Story of Gnostic Illumination

JAMES WASSERMAN

with

KEITH W. STUMP
and HARVEY ROCHMAN

DESTINY BOOKS
Rochester, Vermont • Toronto, Canada

Destiny Books
One Park Street
Rochester, Vermont 05767
www.DestinyBooks.com

Text stock is SFI certified

Destiny Books is a division of Inner Traditions International

Library of Congress Cataloging-in-Publication Data

Names: Wasserman, James, 1948- author. | Stump, Keith W., author. | Rochman, Harvey, author.
Title: Templar heresy : a story of gnostic illumination / James Wasserman with Keith Stump and Harvey Rochman.
Description: Rochester, Vermont : Destiny Books, 2017. | Description based on print version record and CIP data provided by publisher; resource not viewed.
Identifiers: LCCN 2016054445 (print) | LCCN 2017013640 (e-book) | ISBN 9781620556580 (paperback) | ISBN 9781620556597 (e-book)
Subjects: LCSH: Templars—Fiction. | Assassins (Ismailites)—Fiction. | Nizārīs—Fiction. | Albigenses—Fiction. | Islam—Fiction. | Gnosticism—Fiction. | Crusades—Fiction. | Middle Ages—Fiction. | BISAC: FICTION / Historical. | SOCIAL SCIENCE / Freemasonry. | GSAFD: Historical fiction.
Classification: LCC PS3623.A86793 T46 2017 (print) | LCC PS3623.A86793 (e-book) | DDC 813/.6—dc23
LC record available at https://lccn.loc.gov/2016054445

Printed and bound in the United States by Lake Book Manufacturing, Inc. The text stock is SFI certified. The Sustainable Forestry Initiative® program promotes sustainable forest management.

10 9 8 7 6 5 4 3 2 1

Text design and layout by Studio 31

This book was typeset in Adobe Caslon Pro and Trajan Pro

To send correspondence to the author of this book, mail a first-class letter to the author c/o Inner Traditions • Bear & Company, One Park Street, Rochester, VT 05767, and we will forward the communication, or contact the author directly at **http://JamesWassermanBooks.com**.

*This book is dedicated
to those who seek Truth and are
willing to do so on their own terms*

CONTENTS

A Note to the Reader on the Historical Context

This is a story of initiation and the effects of spiritual growth in the personal lives of its main characters. It is also an exploration of the development of the Western Esoteric Tradition through the cultural interaction made possible by the medieval Crusades.

There are several important historical and ideological themes that will help set the stage for what follows, especially some information about the development of Christianity and Islam. We hope the reader's patience during the next few pages will be rewarded with a better insight into our tale.

Constantine I, the Great, embraced Christianity in 312 after a dream on the eve of a decisive military victory that would establish him as the Western Roman emperor. He delayed fully committing himself to his new religion, finally taking baptism on his deathbed in 337. However, in 313, he cosigned the Edict of Milan with the Pagan Eastern Roman emperor, Licinius I. This legalized Christianity, ended the Christian persecutions, and proclaimed tolerance of all faiths.

In 380, Theodosius I declared Christianity the state religion and later issued decrees against the pagan religions. It would remain for Justinian I, however, to fully suppress Paganism. He declared beliefs other than Christianity illegal. He closed the Neoplatonic Academy of Athens in 529, along with other centers of pagan learning and worship. Such enclaves were the repositories of the Hermetic schools of initiation that had evolved from Egypt through Greece to Rome. The dispossessed scholars and mystics took their manuscripts and teachings to Persia, where they were welcomed by the Sassanian dynasty.

In the seventh century, Muhammad preached his unifying vision of monotheism, Islam, in Arabia. His religious revelation was shared with a tribal desert people. Its initial simplicity was to dramatically evolve during the five centuries that precede our story.

The introduction of dissension and the embrace of mystical doctrines began almost immediately after the Prophet's death in 632. Islam was split between Sunnis and Shiites.

The Prophet's father-in-law, Abu Bakr, had led prayers while Muhammad was ill. This encouraged the Sunnis to believe that Muhammad had given Abu Bakr his seal of approval to succeed him and assume the office of Caliph—the leader of Islam after the Prophet's death.

The Shiites, on the other hand, never doubted for an instant that Ali, the Prophet's own cousin and son-in-law, was the person most qualified to receive the spiritual inspiration necessary to lead the faithful. Ali, unlike Abu Bakr, was a member of the *Ahl al-Bayt*, the People of the House, those who shared the Prophet's sacred bloodline.

The Sunnis were the majority party. They looked upon the Caliph as an administrator. The Shia believed the Caliph's most important role was as a religious leader.

A series of disturbing and chaotic events followed over the next half century. Several Caliphs, including Ali, came and went, and a civil war flared between contestants to the Caliphate.

The real cataclysm occurred in 680 when Husayn, the Prophet's grandson, was murdered by the Sunni Caliph. This inexorably alienated the Shia.

Radical religious themes of suffering, expiation, and martyrdom began to be introduced into Shiism. Mystical doctrines developed, such as the concept of a Hidden *Imam*—silently leading righteous Muslims from his invisible throne, inspiring his *dais* (missionary teachers) in the true ways of Islam. Only one Imam served at a time and each was descended from the bloodline of the Prophet. Their role was to prepare humanity for the ultimate appearance of the messianic *Mahdi*, the final Imam, the true Islamic ruler who would open the seventh epoch—as Muhammad had opened the sixth.

✢ ✢ ✢

In 765, a pivotal schism occurred among the Shia. Ismail, the son of the sixth Imam, was supplanted by his younger half-brother as the new seventh Imam. Ismail's followers asserted that the ceremony known as the passing of the *Nass* had already taken place. This mystic blessing from the Imam to his successor opens the psychic pathways of the designated future leader, purifying him for the reception of Truth. The rite irrevocably established the next Imam. Ismail's followers thus proclaimed him the sole, legitimate seventh Imam and broke away from the Shia.

The Shia had already developed a set of clandestine teachings. When the Ismailis splintered off and became even more isolated, they took these hidden doctrines to the next level. Their sense of betrayal led them to formulate ever-stricter interpretations of the intricacies of succession to the Imamate and the proper role of Islam.

The process of acquiring Ismaili knowledge involved the taking of oaths of secrecy, especially as their beliefs grew more exotic. For example: they affirmed an esoteric meaning within the Qur'an that could only be explored with a teacher. One's personal guide would also explain the errors of the majority Sunni and Shia faiths. Students were taught to suspend judgment and orthodoxy in order to discover the inner truth or *batin* concealed within Islam.

Since both Shia and Ismailis grew by conversion—among Greeks, Jews, Sabaeans, Zoroastrians, Gnostics, and others—alien beliefs easily found their way into the evolving Ismaili religious mix.

Many of these will be highlighted in our story.

They include the Hermetic mysteries of Neoplatonism and its emanationist teachings of a spiritual hierarchy and Gnostic angelology. In addition, such traditionally non-Muslim ideas as reincarnation, metempsychosis, divination, and astrology were absorbed.

Numerology was included in the secret curriculum, especially the mysteries of the number seven. While the majority Shia believed in twelve Imams, the Ismailis accepted only seven. The true succession ended with Ismail. He had not died. Rather, he had entered a state of occultation, dwelling in the secret recesses of the world soul, silently guiding his faithful.

Ismail was further conceived as the seventh prophet by whom God revealed Himself to mankind. Adam, Noah, Abraham, Moses, Jesus, and Muhammad preceded him. This doctrine established the Ismailis as *malahida*, heretics, because they acknowledged a prophet following Muhammad—thus violating one of the fundamental tenets of Islam.

The Ismailis successfully established a political state in 909. The Fatimid Dynasty ruled Egypt for some two hundred years. Ismaili ambition had resulted in a secure geographical area where they could teach, study, and practice their faith unmolested by the intolerance of others. The Fatimids built a highly civilized culture, which included a university for the training of dais, known as the *Dar al-Hikma* or House of Wisdom.

By the end of the eleventh century, however, the Fatimids were in decline. Caliph al-Mustansir invoked the power of an Armenian warlord to quell revolts in his kingdom. This was a deal with the devil that resulted in increasing the general's power within the Fatimid state.

Al-Mustansir died in 1094. Since his eldest son, Nizar, had been designated as the spiritual and political heir of his father, the ceremony of the passing of the *Nass* had already occurred.

However, Nizar was denied his rightful position by the general's son, who succeeded his father as Commander of the Armies. Compounding the travesty, Nizar was believed to have been assassinated in 1095 by his younger brother, al-Mustali, who had been recruited into the conspiracy. Al-Mustali was then elevated as the Fatimid Caliph and served as the willing tool of the military dictator.

✤ ✤ ✤

Hasan-i-Sabah (1055–1124) was a Persian Ismaili dai who had completed the course of study in the Dar al-Hikma. By 1090, he had become the Chief Dai of Daylam, a mountainous region of northern Persia, where he established his headquarters at Alamut Castle.

Upon learning of al-Mustansir's death and the efforts to undermine Nizar's Imamate, Hasan worked tirelessly on his behalf. After Nizar's murder, some believed that either Nizar's son or grandson was secretly smuggled to Hasan's care and remained in occultation as the Hidden Imam. Others believed that Nizar had not died, but had clandestinely traveled to Alamut. Hasan was universally acknowledged as the supreme outer head of the Nizari Ismaili movement.

The Nizaris were popularly known as "Hashishim." Historians are divided as to whether they actually used the drug. Some believe they did. Others contend that the term was used by hostile Muslim writers who equated their doctrines and behavior with drunkenness. In either case, Hashishim is the etymological root of our word *assassin,* the more popular name by which the medieval Nizari Ismailis are still known.

Hasan-i-Sabah perfected the art of assassination as a tool of political warfare. His victims were chosen for the pivotal importance they held in the ranks of his enemies. His *fidais* (disciples) would quietly infiltrate the halls of power, in some cases waiting years until summoned by their Master to act. This surprisingly humane tactic resulted in some fifty deaths during the thirty-five years of Hasan's reign. (By way of contrast, during the mid-thirteenth century Mongol invasion of northern Persia, some 80,000 Ismailis were slain in Quhistan in one day.)

In about the year 1100, Hasan sent missionaries to Syria to spread the Nizari Ismaili teachings.

Syria was already a hotbed of heresy, populated by Fatimids,

Qarmatis, Druzes, Nusayris, and Manichaeans. The area's religious diversity was rivaled by a political free-for-all in which various claimants to rulership and dynastic legitimacy divided the land and frequently fought for control. When the Crusaders burst upon the scene in 1097, it only added to the chaos.

The fledgling Syrian Assassin community struggled to survive in their new homeland. They were defeated in battle by the Crusaders in 1106 and again in 1110. A Sunni Seljuk prince destroyed the Assassin community in Aleppo in 1113. They tried to regroup in Damascus where their initial organizing success morphed into failure. In 1128, an anti-Assassin wave arose that killed some 6,000 Nizaris.

In 1132, they tired of trying to establish themselves in urban centers and purchased a fortress in the Nusayri Mountains of western Syria. Over the next seven years, they acquired several more castles. The inaccessible mountain region served as their primary means of defense.

But in 1152, they murdered their first Christian victim. While no motive for that murder has ever been determined, it was a costly move. The Assassins were defeated in battle by the Knights Templar and forced to pay an annual tribute for their continued survival.

The Syrian Assassins were saved from becoming a historical footnote by the leadership of Rashid al-Din Sinan.

TEMPLAR HERESY

A STORY OF
GNOSTIC ILLUMINATION

A silver coin minted at Alamut during the reign
of Imam Muhammad III (r. 1221–1255)
(See afterword for translation)

Marco Polo described a visit to the Alamut region on his way to China in 1271. The Venetian traveler related a story about the Assassins he had heard from several people he met.

Carefully selected young boys from surrounding areas were raised from earliest childhood in the court of the Old Man of the Mountain. They were educated in various languages and customs, courtly etiquette, and trained in martial and other skills. The most talented, courageous, and loyal were then chosen for a unique experience.

During the night, ten or twelve disciples would be drugged with opium and carried unconscious into a hidden area known as the Garden of Delights. It had been constructed to resemble Muhammad's descriptions of Paradise. Beautiful silk tapestries and paintings hung in gilded pavilions. Streams of wine, milk, honey, and cool water flowed through various ducts within the garden. Tasty fruits and elegant and colorful flowers and fragrant plants were carefully cultivated. Couches were laid out for the youths, and here they were entertained by beautiful women, clothed in diaphanous dresses, who sang and danced and initiated them into the arts of love.

The fidais remained in this sensual bliss for four or five days until they were again drugged and carried back to the castle. Upon awakening, they related their experience to the Master. The Old Man explained that he held the keys to Paradise. If they accomplished the mission on which he would be sending them, even if they died, he would summon his angels to transport their souls directly to this heavenly realm.

He then assigned them a target from among his most dangerous enemies. The fervor of his disciples' loyalty was unmatched. Surrounding chieftains and rulers lived in dread of these killers who had no fear of death.

✣ ✣ ✣

On August 12, 1308, Pope Clement V released the articles of accusation against the Knights Templar in a document entitled *Faciens misericordiam*. Among its charges were the following:

- That they worshiped and adored an idol as their God and savior. It was variously described as a human head, or heads, sometimes with three faces, or a human skull. It was believed the idol protected the Order, gave it riches, caused the trees to flower and the land to germinate.
- That in their receptions, they surrounded the idol with a small cord that they then wore at all times around their waists in veneration of the idol.
- That at the ceremony of reception, the Order demanded its new members deny Christ, or Christ crucified, sometimes Jesus, God, the Virgin, or the Saints.
- That at the ceremony of reception, the candidate was told to spit on the cross, or an image of the cross, or of Jesus. That they sometimes trampled the cross underfoot, or urinated upon it, both at the reception ceremony and at other times.
- That the Order taught that Jesus was not the true God, that he was a false prophet, that he had not suffered on the cross, that he had died not for the redemption of humanity but for his own sins, that neither the receptor nor the candidate could expect salvation through Jesus.
- That they did not believe in the sacraments of the Church.
- That there were a series of kisses during the ceremony of reception, by the candidate or by the receptor, either on the other's mouth, navel, bare stomach, buttocks, base of the spine, or penis.
- That they conducted all their business in secret meetings and at night and that all the above errors could only flourish because of this secrecy.

PART ONE

THE QIYAMA AND THE ASSASSINS

✠

CHAPTER 1

Saturday, the 17th of Ramadan, 559 A.H. (August 8, 1164), was a brilliantly clear morning. Alamut Castle, the headquarters of the Assassin Order, sat upon a rock some 650 feet high, overlooking a valley in the rugged Elburz Mountains of northern Persia near the Caspian Sea.

A large crowd stood in the courtyard of the fortress and cheered, their swords raised high. They were assembled in ranks, their white robes dazzling in the sun. Banners of white, red, yellow, and green rippled in the wind under the blue sky.

Upon a high dais stood a fervent figure, tall, handsome, bearded, wearing a white turban and robe. He was Hasan II, the thirty-seven-year-old Grand Master of the Assassin Order. He ascended the *minbar* (pulpit) at noon and raised his arms toward heaven. His back was turned to Mecca.

His noble face shining with confidence and wisdom, Hasan gestured for silence. He then delivered the heretical *Qiyama* proclamation that abolished Islamic religious law in favor of a more mystical approach to spirituality.

He was jubilant, in an ecstatic state of revelation and inspiration, and his words would have repercussions through the ages.

"In the name of Allah, the merciful, the compassionate. This is the day of Qiyama, the Day of Resurrection! Today, we rise to a new state of being. Today we rejoin the Divine, the Eternal Light. Today we enter Paradise!

"By proclamation of the Hidden One, the invisible Imam, we are now free from the shackles of religion. The chains of restriction are struck from our necks! A New Age begins.

"This day we discard all external forms of worship. We turn from the outward forms of religion—from the letter of the law—to the inner meaning of the commandments, the *batin*, the hidden depths of inner truth."

Hasan raised his arms toward the sun.

"Today we stand in the light of God! Rejoice, my people, in your liberty! Abandon the fast! Remove the veil! Drink wine!

"No longer do we turn toward Mecca—for all the earth is illuminated by the light of God! We have risen. We are free. There is no law beyond Do what thou wilt! Praise be to God, Lord of the worlds!"

Hasan looked skyward, his eyes shining, his face beatific.

The crowd broke into thunderous applause that echoed through the valley. The people's love for their Imam had been fulfilled by this revolutionary proclamation. Such courage! Elders proudly remembered Hasan-i-Sabah's creative political and religious consolidation decades earlier. He had elevated the Nizari Ismailis to the vanguard of Islamic thought. They now recognized the same genius in their new leader.

Many Assassins had tired of the conservative stance of Hasan-i-Sabah's successor, Buzurgumid, Hasan II's grandfather. Yes, he was a great general and had expanded the Nizari territory. In addition to his military campaigns, there had been several high-profile assassinations, including that of the illegitimate Fatimid Caliph himself. But compared to Hasan-i-Sabah's revolutionary energy, Buzurgumid proved to be an unexciting and uninspiring leader. His son, Muhammad, Hasan II's father, was even worse. He had remained virtually dormant during his twenty-four year reign, avoiding any active expansion of territory. He had chosen instead to rest on the laurels of his father. A longing for Alamut's earlier glory was widespread.

The young Hasan II had long been regarded as the answer to their frustration. He was believed to be an extraordinary soul. Rumors had swirled for years that he was actually the secret son of the Hidden Imam himself. His Qiyama proclamation this day seemed to hint at that possibility. It was certainly proof of his remarkable stature as a spiritual visionary. Imagine overturning five centuries of Islamic law in one afternoon! And to do so here, at Alamut! The chests of his supporters swelled with pride at the thought that their Imam had reclaimed the preeminent position of the Assassin community as the religious leaders of the entire Islamic world.

While there was great enthusiasm on the faces of most of the people in the courtyard, yet a few men were hiding their discomfort. They cast quick glances at their confederates, then swiftly lowered their eyes. They were seething with hatred for the blasphemy to which they had been exposed this day.

The teachings of the Prophet Muhammad were absolutely clear. In fact, they had been collected in writing and taught by generations of religious leaders. The Muslim faithful had followed the Prophet's example and advice in their daily lives for longer than half a millennium. There was no room for doubt when it came to the proper rules of behavior for a Muslim. Whether it was one's conduct in marriage, the foods one should eat, how to dress, how to bathe, how to raise children, how and when to pray and perform the other duties of the faith, how a leader should administer the affairs of the community—all were carefully spelled out.

Allah's rules had been dictated to His Messenger by the Archangel Gabriel. These precepts and codes had stood the test of time because they worked—and they worked because they came directly from God.

Drink wine? Break the Ramadan fast? Who did this madman think he was? They would quietly and carefully seek out their fellow Assassin dissenters and make their next plans together. The Qiyama heresy would not stand here at Alamut or survive to spread anywhere else. This *mulhid* (apostate) must be stopped. It was that simple.

CHAPTER 2

Later that night Hasan was with his friend and favorite student, the young Rashid al-Din Sinan. Twenty-four years old, with jet-black hair and beard, Sinan displayed the lean intensity of the committed mystic. He deeply admired and loved his teacher. They walked together in the now-empty courtyard of Alamut. As they gazed upon the starlit heaven, Hasan further expounded his new doctrine of spiritual liberation.

"We have a divine mission, Sinan. Our destinies are linked. There is a New Dispensation! We are free of slavery and restriction. Now we will experience God within!"

He paused so that Sinan could absorb these unfamiliar and revolutionary concepts. Hasan was keenly aware of how shocking the Qiyama proclamation was, even to so supportive an ally as Sinan. Hasan knew that Islam was an extremely rigid and stylized religion. He knew that his Qiyama doctrine would be considered heretical by even the most tolerant Muslim.

He continued with the impassioned tone of a prophet, "Our people must understand that spirituality goes beyond religion, Sinan. Obedience to Allah begins in the heart and mind. True worship is the ecstatic celebration of God."

Hasan removed his outer robe. "Like this mantle; the outward observances of religion are merely a cloak for powerful inner truths. All else is irrelevant."

To underline his point, he threw the cloak to the ground with disdain.

The loyal Sinan was troubled. He sensed the hidden currents of hatred swirling within the Assassin community. Several friends had confided in him after the gathering that day. They had warned him of the discontent already voiced by some against the Qiyama.

"My lord Hasan . . . Many beyond our camp will call us heretics and blasphemers. Even some of our own people will reject us."

"They are the unbelievers, Sinan. They cling to illusions. They bow their necks to the yoke of a slave religion."

"But their passions have been stirred. They may be small in number, my Teacher, but their fervor makes them dangerous."

"Sinan, we follow the will of Allah. The revelations I shared with everyone this day were those that Allah shared with me!"

Sinan was moved by his Master's courage and inspired by the certainty and self-confidence of his mystical proclamation.

"These powerful inner truths . . . How can I know them?"

Hasan was delighted. "I will show you, Sinan. And you will come to know their power. That power lies within you—ready to be awakened. Even now it stirs!

"And when you have known it and are ready to speak it forth, you will take the new doctrine beyond this land. The light that burns in you will shine into Syria, and from there will illumine the entire world. This is a teaching for all peoples. One day, all men and all women will live in the Light of Inner Truth!"

CHAPTER 3

Two years after Hasan II's Qiyama proclamation, Sinan had truly fulfilled the hopes of his mentor and friend. He had made rapid progress in his spiritual practices. Sinan had attained to the state that Hasan had promised—Gnosis—the knowledge of God within. He had come to a position of certainty, not faith. Sinan was in communication with his own unconscious and thus able to experience intuitive understanding. He had developed a mastery over his own thought process, possessing the ability to direct and hold his attention to specific ideas and images. He had learned to focus himself on specific spiritual energies and to project his consciousness into chosen regions of the higher planes. Sinan was able thereby to refine and enhance his own psychic energies and to develop greater clarity about his personal mission.

Sinan's point of view had expanded to encompass alternate possibilities in every event and to perceive a unity underlying creation. He knew himself to be a player in the universal drama. He understood this to be as much a crucial necessity of the utmost seriousness as it was simultaneously a fanciful and comical diversion in the mind of his Creator. Sinan felt himself to be at one with the true purpose of his earthly incarnation and untroubled by the apparent contradictions such deeper and complex understanding had revealed.

The second part of Sinan's task—as discussed during that fateful evening's conversation two years before—was the carrying forth of the Qiyama message into Syria. Hasan II would appoint his most successful disciple as the Chief Dai of the Syrian Nizari community.

Sinan left Alamut and traveled by caravan on the long and treacherous route south and westward toward Syria. The dusty traveling party pushed on through the Elburz Mountains and emerged onto the Iranian Plateau. They crossed over the Zagros Mountains until they reached Mesopotamia. They forded the Tigris and Euphrates rivers and continued into the Syrian Desert. The mountains of western Syria rose before them at the end of a two-and-a-half-month trek.

Sinan was welcomed by the tenuous Assassin community in the Nusayri Mountains along the northern Mediterranean coast of Syria. The Syrian Assassins had struggled since the first missionaries sent by Hasan-i-Sabah arrived from Alamut around the year 1100. Even after abandoning their original efforts to build urban communities in Aleppo and Damascus (which had resulted in the mass slaughter of their people), they faced severe challenges in the more-isolated mountain home to which they had fled in 1132. Between the greater Sunni population and the European Crusaders, theirs was a fight for survival. Sinan's easy manner, and the fervor and intelligence he radiated, rapidly confirmed Hasan II's wisdom in appointing his young friend as the leader of this regional group.

Sinan now stood upon a dais at Al-Kaph, the mountain headquarters of the Syrian branch of the Order. He was in the middle of his first major sermon to his new followers, reasserting the proclamation of the Qiyama made earlier by Imam Hasan II at Alamut. Sinan radiated charisma and authority.

"Today we rise into the world of Light! Today we begin a journey of discovery—the search for God within. What wonders we shall see on this path!"

The crowd cheered wildly. Their religious intoxication was mirrored in the state of ecstasy revealed upon Sinan's face.

The power of a unified belief was the beginning of a period of political stability their new chief would bring to Syria.

CHAPTER 4

Sinan's leadership of the Syrian Assassins—headquartered at Al-Kaph, Masyaf, and the other regional fortresses—led to a period of growth and prosperity that remained undiminished throughout his lifetime.

Yet the position of the Nizari apostates was always precarious, particularly in the beginning; Sinan immediately faced serious challenges from two Sunni warrior chieftains. The first was the great Zangid general Nur al-Din, who made his headquarters in Aleppo. He was a mighty conqueror whose fervent Sunni faith served to set him squarely against the Assassin heretics.

Nur al-Din's elevation of his Kurdish general, Saladin, to the rulership of Egypt—and the latter's destruction of the Fatimid Dynasty—also bode ill for Sinan. Saladin was inspired with a holy fervor for Muslim unity that could only be compared to that shown by the Prophet himself. Saladin's intelligence, righteousness, and military skill were unrivaled. His rejection of the Shiite and Ismaili heresies posed a formidable challenge to Sinan's survival. Saladin was ever convinced he bore the sword of righteousness. And Sinan and his Assassin heretics would be spared no mercy by that sword.

In addition, Sinan had to deal with local Nusayri tribal groups, mountain marauders, and assorted vigilantes. The fierceness and unpredictability of these groups made them dangerous to all.

Upon Nur al-Din's death in 1174, Saladin proclaimed his independence from the Zangid Dynasty and established his Ayyubid line, which ruled Egypt until 1249. Saladin next projected his military might into Syria and throughout the Mideast.

He proved to be Sinan's most dangerous foe—until they reached an accord.

During Saladin's siege of the Assassin castle of Masyaf, a messenger from Sinan arrived at the sultan's court asking to speak with Saladin privately. Saladin cleared his court of all but two trusted Mameluke guards. The messenger asked why the great sultan would not ask these two men to leave.

Saladin explained. "I regard these two as my sons. They and I are one."

The messenger then asked the guards what they would do if he told them Sinan wished them to kill Saladin.

They drew their swords and answered, "Command us as you wish."

There is no further indication of any hostility between Saladin and Sinan.

CHAPTER 5

Sinan's reputation for integrity and skill grew during the decades of his reign. He was regarded, even by his enemies, as a man of honor. His Nizari heresy aside, regional Muslim leaders were forced to admire the competence with which he advanced the interests of his people.

It was now the year 1201. Sinan, in his sixties, sat in meditation, cross-legged and motionless on the marble floor of his high balcony overlooking the courtyard.

Below him Aisha, a servant girl new to Al-Kaph, put down a heavy basket that she might rest. The old woman with her also stopped, but was impatient. Aisha looked up at the dazzling white-robed figure sitting on the balcony.

She was curious and asked the old woman, "Why does our lord Sinan sit on his balcony for hours without moving?"

The reply was disinterested, "It is said that he looks within."

This intrigued Aisha. "What do you mean?"

"What am I—a scholar? No more foolish questions! Help me carry this inside."

At sunset that evening Aisha entered Sinan's chambers carrying a silver tray bearing assorted fruits, which she placed on a low table next to the cushions on the floor. Tapestries rippled in the evening breeze.

Sinan was standing at the window, staring into the setting sun. Aisha noticed him and froze, painfully aware of her intrusion. Sinan turned and acknowledged her presence with a nod.

"You have a question. Ask it."

Aisha hesitated, looked down, then asked nervously, "What do you see inside yourself when you sit all day without moving?"

Sinan disregarded the question. "Why do you not look at me when you speak?"

Aisha hesitated, then replied with embarrassment, "You will see what I am, my lord."

Sinan turned and looked back into the sun, pausing for what felt to Aisha like an eternity.

"I see a woman, discarded, destitute, carrying a dead child, walking on the Hama road, thinking how to take her own life."

Aisha's head snapped up, astonished. She gasped.

Sinan continued gently, "Many are the roads that lead here. What is important is that you are here now, not what brought you here."

Tears flowed down Aisha's cheeks. Sinan walked over to a basin of water, picked up a sponge, dipped it in the water, wrung it out, and gently wiped her face. He took a rose from a vase, handed it to her, then bent down and kissed her on the forehead. As he did these things, he quoted an Arab proverb.

"A sponge to wipe out the past, a rose to make the present sweet, and a kiss to salute the future."

Aisha searched his face, her eyes bright with tears.

PART TWO

The Mission of the Templars

CHAPTER 6

Three years later some twenty men on horseback ascended a path along the rugged Nusayri Mountains. They were a Crusader delegation on their way to Al-Kaph. The morning air was bracing, easing their breathing as they climbed, the elevation providing a refreshing change from their ride along the Mediterranean coast after having left the hills of Jerusalem two weeks earlier. The year was 1204.

The group was led by Henry of Champagne, king of Jerusalem, a beleaguered Crusader territory since the successful campaign of 1099 over a century before. Surrounded on all sides by the indigenous Infidel, Christian survival demanded alliances. Although Henry was only thirty-one, his careworn face was evidence of the burden of a tragic early maturity.

The Christian king was here to reach out to Sinan, whom he recognized as king of the Assassins. Henry knew the Assassins were regarded as apostates by both Sunni and Shia Muslims alike. Hated outcasts themselves, perhaps they would be willing to talk with the equally despised Crusaders.

Henry was acutely aware of the danger he faced during this mission. His predecessor, Conrad of Montferrat, had been slain two years earlier by Assassin fidais. Henry's uncle, King Richard the Lionhearted, immediately arranged for Henry to be married to Isabel, Conrad's widow, thus establishing Henry's claim to the Jerusalem throne.

Dark rumors still swirled suggesting that Richard had contracted with the Assassins for Conrad's murder. People suspected Richard's alliance with Saladin may have led to a secret relationship with Sinan. While Richard had never discussed this with his nephew, Henry almost hoped it was true. If it were, perhaps he and his men would be safe. It might also mean he could be dealing with someone who would be willing to negotiate across cultural boundaries.

✞ ✞ ✞

Among Henry's group were several members of the Knights
Templar Order. Formed in 1119 after the massacre of some sixty
Christians en route to Jerusalem, the original nine knights had
been granted lodging in the Al-Aqsa mosque on the Temple
Mount. They were charged with the protection of European pilgrims visiting the Holy Land—the birthplace of their religion
and their savior.

The Order enjoyed a meteoric rise to prominence after
being sponsored by Bernard of Clairvaux, the widely respected
Cistercian religious leader. Under Bernard's patronage, the
Templars had been recognized as an official body of the Catholic
Church in 1128.

Bernard's concept of the Holy Warrior took flight. This was
a new idea for Christianity, although its roots extended back to
the biblical King David. The Knights Templar combined the
chivalry of the medieval knight with the cloistered vows of the
monk. Bernard had created an entirely unique Rule that dictated
their behavior down to the smallest detail. Knight/Monks, they
were equally skilled with weapons as they were observant in their
religious duties.

Among the Templars was a young warrior named Roland de
Provence. He was twenty-five and dressed in the characteristic
white robe of the Order. The red cross on his chest had been
awarded the Templars in 1147. Roland's childhood friend and
fellow Templar, Andre d'Avignon, some two years his junior,
rode up next to him. As their Rule stipulated, both men were
bearded with close-cropped hair. Roland's was black, Andre's a
muted brown.

Andre prattled on with childlike enthusiasm.

"The Assassins—Nizari Ismailis—have ten fortresses
and 60,000 men at arms. They're counted as heretics by most
Saracens, but are greatly feared by everyone. Many enemies have
died by their daggers, yet they never harm women or children.

Even Saladin feared them, and made a truce. And now, our brave King Henry seeks an alliance."

Roland looked straight ahead, showing no interest, but the talkative Andre continued enthusiastically.

"It's said that the Old Man of the Mountain—that's what they call their leader Sinan—possesses ancient wisdom. That he can intuit men's thoughts and see the future. That he can read letters without opening them, converse with snakes, move things with his mind, that . . ."

Roland cut him off. "Enough, Andre! Superstitious nonsense!"

Roland spurred his horse ahead. He'd heard enough.

His irritation was amplified manyfold by his Templar commander, Guillaume de Gonneville. At age forty-five, Guillaume was the oldest man in the Crusader party. His was a severe and humorless countenance, born of an excess of self-denial. Victim of a strong nature suppressed by an indomitable will, Guillaume was a man at war with himself and his world. He was as confident in his stubbornness as he was plagued by rage and insecurity.

Guillaume rode up next to King Henry to repeat his concerns for the mission at hand. The king was well aware of Guillaume's ferocity and martial skill as well as the obedience of his soldiers. While Guillaume was a harsh leader, the discipline he demanded of his men was of unquestionable value in a dangerous land.

"My Liege. May I speak freely?"

"Of course, Guillaume."

"These fiends can never be trusted to honor a truce. They are murderers. They are our enemies and the enemies of Christ."

Henry paused to contemplate the difference between his concerns as a king and the relative freedom offered Guillaume by the extent of his hatred. He perceived an almost admirable simplicity in the fanatic's worldview.

"I understand your concerns, Guillaume. If we can avoid

engaging with them while we defend Jerusalem, it is worth the risk. One less enemy to fight. The Assassins can serve as a balance against our mutual foes. We will seek a peace with them that benefits us both."

Mortified by the thought of being in an alliance with heretics, Guillaume exploded.

"Sire, these animals are not fit even to receive you!"

"Silence! My course is clear."

The men continued their climb up the long mountain path.

CHAPTER 7

Poised on the crest of a tall mountain peak, Al-Kaph was Sinan's favored headquarters. The Crusaders had been at the fortress for several days. Henry and Sinan's discussions and negotiations revealed the advantages they each would gain from a peace between themselves. Now that the Christian legation was soon to return to Jerusalem, a celebratory banquet had been arranged for the evening.

The Crusaders and a group of Assassin warriors filled the castle's torch-lit banquet hall where the guests were being fêted in traditional Oriental fashion. The stone walls of the room were hung with colorful tapestries that glowed in the candlelight. Smoke from the *bakhoor* incense piles filled the room with a pleasing scent. The diners reclined on great cushions. They were being served by young fidais whose training included mastery of the nuances of courtly etiquette. Jugglers with fiery torches provided entertainment during the dinner.

With flowing gray hair and lengthy beard, Sinan radiated charismatic wisdom and serenity as he reclined on the cushions next to King Henry. The Old Man of the Mountain seemed every inch the perfect host and leader. He leaned toward Henry.

"Is the food to your satisfaction, noble guest?"

"Indeed, sir! I admit that I am delighted to find myself sitting here with you tonight given the history of our two peoples."

"Within the precincts of this camp, all divisions are forgotten, and all dwell in peace and fraternity."

Henry raised his drink and called out to his men.

"Raise your goblets in a toast to our august host!"

The Crusaders did so.

At this moment, the beautiful Aisha entered the room full of men. Roland was startled by the raw sensuality and power she quietly exuded. Olive-skinned with jet-black hair and dark eyes,

Aisha made brief eye contact with Roland as she served Sinan. Slightly older than the Templar knight, Aisha walked over and stood next to him.

"Welcome to the domain of the True Self."

Roland was stunned and confused. He was angry that a woman would have the effrontery to approach and speak directly to him. It was a violation of Bernard's carefully crafted Templar Rule to speak to women or be in their company, other than blood relatives. But he was a young, healthy male and absolutely smitten by her.

Searching for some defense against his instinctual fires, he proclaimed, "In my country, women do not approach men."

To which Aisha coyly replied, "And that pleases you?"

Roland was flustered. This was an entirely new set of feelings for him, and he was helpless. The ascetic monasticism of his Order, with its harsh prohibitions against contact with the opposite sex, had generally been successful in restraining his wandering eye. Aisha threatened him with her boldness. His attraction to her was an unfamiliar, uncomfortable, and disconcerting sensation. It left him floundering for self-control in the face of the vulnerability she exposed.

Guillaume, seeing them standing next to each other, radiated disapproval and hostility.

Meanwhile, Henry and Sinan continued their exchange of diplomatic niceties, seemingly unaware of the tense scene playing out near them.

"The fearlessness of your fidais is renowned throughout the world."

Sinan replied in a matter-of-fact manner, "Each disciple has faced his worst fear and overcome it. The weapons of man no longer hold dread."

Puzzled, Henry asked, "What do you mean?"

"Each man is guided into the depths of his soul to discover his greatest fear, to taste it, to confront it, and to overcome it."

"How is such magic accomplished?"

"It cannot be explained; it can only be experienced." Sinan paused. The room had become quiet as the other diners attended to this conversation. Even the jugglers paused.

"Do any of your men have the courage to face such an ordeal?"

The Templars gazed nervously at each other. There were no takers. Finally, Roland rose and stepped forward to save face for the Crusaders.

Sinan whispered something to Aisha, the word *hashish* being discernible. She left the room.

Henry was relieved that one of his men had answered the challenge, but concerned because of his fondness for Roland—and the strange and mysterious nature of this fierce mountain king.

"This is Roland de Provence, one of my most trusted knights."

Sinan looked with benevolence upon Roland. Then he spoke firmly to the young Crusader. His piercing eyes held those of the Templar knight with an intensity that seemed to belie the gentleness of his next words.

"This ordeal is not to be undertaken lightly, my son. It is not the way of you Franks. There is no dishonor in withdrawing."

"I am a Templar, my lord, in service to Christ, the Pope, and King Henry. A Templar is no stranger to facing his fears."

Aisha returned with a cup, which she handed to Roland. Sinan assured his guest he was aware of the universal laws of honor and hospitality.

"Drink this. On my word as your host, you will not be harmed by it."

Roland paused for a moment, looking again into Sinan's eyes, then drained the cup.

Sinan turned to King Henry and said, "This is a private

matter. I will attend to him. Later, if he chooses, he will speak to you of the experience."

As he rose, Sinan addressed the Crusaders. "Please continue. Enjoy the feast!"

The jugglers resumed their act. Sinan, Roland, and Aisha left the hall as Andre looked on with concern.

CHAPTER 8

A small room, well away from the noise of the banquet, was lit by candles. Roland reclined on cushions. Sinan sat across from him, holding a twisting, snake-shaped wand with the head of a lion carved on its top. Aisha stood in the shadows, although Roland was quite conscious of her. The desires she had awakened in him had overtaken his best efforts to either ignore or deny.

But even his confused passion for this woman seemed to be receding as the initial effects of the potion gradually took effect. It began with a feeling of lightness that evolved into a sensation of overall well-being. His senses became stimulated and more responsive to the subtleties of light and color, the texture of the fabric of the pillows, a growing lassitude in his limbs—while his consciousness seemed to become independent of its normal connection to his body and brain.

Even though he knew he was becoming increasingly disoriented, his mental and emotional state remained calm. There was an unfamiliar sense of ease. Roland was enchanted by this heightened sensory awareness.

As the drug continued to pervade Roland's body, Sinan could feel Roland's increasing suggestibility. The adept began to ever-so-slightly rotate the lion-headed snake wand in his hands. Roland gazed at the sinuous curves of the snake's body as it seemed to entwine around itself in an undulating motion, alive yet non-threatening. Roland entered the deeper realms of his own creative consciousness.

Sinan began to guide Roland on an internal journey. His words came slowly and hypnotically, and his voice was calculated to initially convey confidence and safety to the young mind sitting opposite him.

"The light is fading now. You are journeying into a dark place, walking alone, calmly and confidently enjoying the silent shadows of the night."

The Master's timing was perfect. Through long experience he had caught Roland at exactly the right moment in the cycle of the drug's effect. Roland's defenses had been assuaged and his mind was attuned to the gently spoken guiding words.

Roland envisioned himself in a dark and featureless landscape, deep in a velvet night. He was walking alone with a sense of solitude and peace, as if he had moved far beyond the cares of his everyday responsibilities in the social world he inhabited. He was aware of a freedom, a lack of expectations, the absence of judgments from observers. The beauty of the stars, brightening the night sky with their innumerable points of brilliance, was almost sensuous.

Yet, without explanation or warning, gradually at first, an alarm began to sound in the deeper regions of Roland's mind. A sense of unwellness, of dislocation and imbalance, began to arise. Perhaps it was not yet a feeling of personal peril, but a look of uncertainty and distress grew on his face.

Sinan had sought this precise effect. He knew the deceptively simple snake-shaped wand would provide a psychological trigger of danger to one raised on the precepts of the Bible with its curse against the serpent. Sinan's voice, still calm, became firmer, more measured. A tinge of menace began to color his tone. He started to lead Roland further into the depths of a repressed psyche through a series of increasingly threatening and gloomy images.

"The darkness begins to press in on you. An unfamiliar premonition passes over you. You are feeling a devouring gulf of despair. Your body tightens, your breath quickens, your heart pounds against your chest."

Roland started moving rapidly in his mind's eye. Panic beset him. Sweat began to bead on his face. He felt a terror penetrating into his heart, rendering him powerless before the Enemy of his own imagining.

"And now, before you, like a vast dark cloud, rises your secret fear. Quickly! It comes closer! There is no exit."

Roland felt himself running as a demonic cloud of infinite darkness with leering malevolent eyes began to form in front of him in whatever direction he turned—enveloping him in rhythm with Sinan's hypnotic narration.

"You are powerless before the terror, the horror you refuse to face, the hidden private dread from which you have tried to escape your entire life."

Roland was overwhelmed with the recognition of an emptiness at the very core of what he believed to have been himself—a nothingness that lay at what he used to conceive as his center.

The utter horror of this state of absence, of non-being, was paralyzing. He desperately wished to be able to avoid it, but was cornered, trapped. There was no means to defend against it. It was as if the illusion of his self had been shattered forever. Where could he hide from the naked truth of his innermost reality?

Sinan studied Roland with the utterly focused eyes of a tiger stalking its prey.

"But the running is over now. The great fear surrounds you, envelops you, engulfs you, and you know it for what it is. You look into its eyes—and it looks back!"

Sinan placed his hands on Roland's head, closed his eyes, and read Roland's thoughts. After a few moments, Roland convulsed and collapsed into unconsciousness. Aisha moved to his side, lifting his head into her lap as she soothed his brow with a damp cloth.

CHAPTER 9

Early the next morning, Henry and Sinan walked together through the courtyard in conversation. The Crusaders were preparing for their departure.

The feeling that they had bridged their vast differences to attain a common aim during this mission filled Henry with a sense of relief and ease. He looked up at two high towers just ahead. On each tower stood a sentinel clad in a white tunic with a red sash, wearing red boots.

In the spirit of their more relaxed cordiality, Henry commented on the discipline of Sinan's fidais.

"Your men are to be commended for their attention to duty in this fierce heat."

"These men obey me far better than Christians obey their lords."

Henry was surprised and reacted defensively to the criticism in Sinan's statement.

"Sir, my men are loyal and fully trustworthy!"

Sinan looked up and gave a signal with his hand. The two fidais immediately flung themselves from the towers, falling a great distance to their deaths.

Henry was mortified by this gruesome demonstration of obedience. He crossed himself reflexively and proclaimed his disgust, "Dear God! Barbaric savagery!"

Sinan replied with equanimity and a measured calm in his tone, "They know that they do not die. There is only life in other forms."

Henry was thoroughly shaken by this incident. His years in the Holy Land had exposed the French nobleman to a great deal of behavior that was different from anything he had ever witnessed or imagined in Europe. But a double suicide, produced by the wave of a hand and a nod of the head, was incomprehensible to him. He was rendered speechless.

The door to Henry's newly minted feelings of kinship with his host slammed shut. As Henry again remembered King Conrad's murder at the hands of the Assassins, he plunged into a series of dark and conflicting emotions—respect mingled with fear, even loathing. Henry was thus more susceptible than he otherwise might have been to Sinan's next request, which caught the troubled king off guard.

"My friend, I would ask a favor of you—that the knight called Roland be allowed to remain here as a liaison, your personal representative to my court."

Although reeling from what he had just witnessed, Henry thought for a long moment. The advantages to this course of action were so obvious it was immediately tempting to agree. The entire purpose of his mission to the Assassin headquarters had been to form an alliance and gain a better understanding of the regional and religious dynamics of the Saracen enemy. Sunni, Shia, Nizari were all concepts far from the Roman Catholic king's experience, yet he knew them to be the lifeblood and lever of his survival in this mysterious land.

Henry knew Roland to be an intelligent and perceptive young man. In fact, Roland and Henry's parents had been longtime friends. The king and the Templar had thus known each other since childhood, when they played together as boys during their parents' visits to each other's estates.

The king admired the younger knight's courage and resourcefulness. But this was a dangerous and strange land; Henry was concerned for the well-being of anyone in his care.

"Roland's father is an important nobleman of France, and one of my closest friends. I would require a firm assurance of his safety here."

Sinan nodded in affirmation.

Henry knew the word of a potential long-term ally was never given lightly.

"But even with such assurance, I think it's a decision Roland must make for himself."

Sinan nodded. "I agree."

CHAPTER 10

Later that day, Henry and Guillaume were in an animated conversation in the visitors' quarters of the castle. After some few hours of reflection, Henry was even more favorable to the idea of Roland remaining behind as a representative of the Crusader kingdom. He genuinely believed the lack of knowledge of these disparate peoples could be remedied by closer physical contact. The responsibilities of Jerusalem called for his own departure, of course, but if he were to have his choice of a diplomat to this strange new ally, he could find no better candidate than Roland. The Templar's intelligence, trustworthiness, and loyalty could not be questioned.

Henry was also aware that a relationship between the young knight and the foreign king formed during their strange interlude during the banquet. While neither discussed details with him, the time they spent together and Sinan's surprising request indicated some affinity.

Guillaume, as might be expected, was visibly upset.

Raised in a religious household, Guillaume had nurtured an angry pride in his Christian faith. He remembered the armed men on horseback riding through his family's estate in France as they passed on their long journey to the Holy Land. Some would stop and talk to the boy, extolling the glories they anticipated in battling and defeating the Saracen Infidel. The sight of their armor and lances, their swords and visors, the huge horses on which they rode that were covered with metal. The beasts seemed to breathe fire through their nostrils. Guillaume's imagination was filled with thoughts of battle and glory as he too slayed the enemies of his Savior.

As Guillaume grew older and his faith matured, his body hardened as he relentlessly pushed himself to master the craft of knighthood. He served as a squire under the tutelage of mentors who shaped his skills in fighting, the use of arms, and horsemanship. Guillaume fueled his determination to meet the challenges of his probation with thoughts of later glory. He knew he would enter the sacred brotherhood of knighthood, undergo that religious and feudal ceremony to his liege lord, and become a warrior. He, too, would meet all challenges with honor and steel.

Fiery preachers filled him with a hatred of sin that came quite naturally to him. He began to see his knightly calling as a personal means by which he could combat evil. When he read Bernard of Clairvaux's letter *In Praise of the New Knighthood*, in which the Holy Warrior is described in detail, Guillaume understood his future lay within the Knights Templar Order.

Bernard's words still resonated within him. "This new Order of knights is one that is unknown by the ages. They fight two wars, one against adversaries of flesh and blood, and another against a spiritual army of wickedness in the heavens."

How could he understand such an eloquent call to defeat the very concept of evil with the idea of King Henry forming a political alliance with the Infidel? By definition, he understood Sinan and the Assassins to be the very enemies of his Savior, those whom Bernard called wicked.

In addition, Guillaume was certainly not fond of Roland. He despised him for his calm and easy social manner, the kind of foppery that had no place in a military order. Roland's conversation with the Assassin whore the other night was a case in point. Guillaume hated the company of women. Warned by both scripture and the words of the Templar Rule, he understood the female as the Devil's hand extended to encourage sin.

He knew of Henry's friendship with Roland's family and that, too, caused him jealousy. Certainly Roland's parents' wealth exceeded that of Guillaume's family, but Guillaume's years of sacrifice and leadership should have made up for any lack of "breeding." God, how he hated these pampered young men and their openness to the strange and intoxicating ways of the Holy Land.

When Henry told him of Sinan's offer, Guillaume exploded, "My Liege, this is a bad idea! Roland should not be left alone here."

"He will not be alone, Guillaume. If Roland agrees to stay, I will leave Pierre Duchien here to serve as his ally and assistant."

While Guillaume was mortified by this entire plan, he realized he was powerless to change the king's decision. He accepted the fact that Duchien would be a good choice for a bad assignment. Closer in age to Guillaume, Pierre Duchien was a Templar sergeant who had served the Order for over twenty years. With such a stalwart guide keeping an eye on Roland, perhaps King Henry's folly could be rendered at least less dangerous.

CHAPTER 11

A servant showed Roland into the library. The room was filled with books and artifacts neatly organized on shelves. Manuscript scrolls were carefully arranged and methodically stored so they could be easily and safely identified and accessed. As Roland waited, he examined some manuscripts laid out on the main table.

When Sinan entered, Roland looked up and yet avoided making eye contact. Sinan was the first to speak.

"I have asked King Henry to allow you to remain here as his personal liaison to my court. He leaves the decision to you."

Roland continued to look down and away from the turbaned Master of Al-Kaph. He was embarrassed because of his weakness the previous night, more so because he knew that Sinan had read his innermost fears during their session.

"Do not feel ashamed, my son. You experienced for the first time the great emptiness at the center of yourself—the terrifying void of nothingness that lies at the heart of all being. This is the universal darkness that can only be filled by the Light of God. Yet you fear there is no God, no afterlife, no meaning."

This caused Roland to look directly into Sinan's eyes. It was one thing to know that someone has seen your innermost thoughts. It was quite another to hear them repeated back to you aloud.

Sinan continued.

"It's only natural that you have such doubts. Your belief in God is just that—a belief without substance or foundation."

He paused as Roland gave him a quizzical gaze. Sinan continued with firmness. "Believe nothing until you have discovered it for yourself through your own experience."

Roland was dismissive. "How can a mere man experience God?"

"Would you like to find out?"

CHAPTER 12

The Crusaders were in the courtyard attending to their final preparations to depart. Aisha approached Roland, but stopped some distance from the cluster of Christian warriors. Roland saw her and walked over.

She whispered privately, "My lord Sinan commands me to give you a message." She paused for emphasis and continued, "The dawn does not come twice to awaken a man."

Roland looked up and in the distance saw the white-robed figure of Sinan standing motionless on the high balcony. Roland looked back at Aisha, her eyes shining. She smiled at him—an intimate smile, filled with brightness . . . and promise.

Roland at last shook off the doubts and anticipation that had plagued him since his conversation with Sinan in the library. He understood at the deepest level that there was something here meant specifically for him. That this unexpected detour was actually the next step on the path of his life. He had only to have the courage to face the thought of leaving his past behind and to trust his instincts about this strange man—a man whose alarming power had already placed him far from anything or anyone he had yet experienced.

Roland approached King Henry to confirm the king's desires and the utility of his remaining behind in this exotic realm. They spoke out of earshot of the other men. The king nodded.

"I hope you will be able to help us keep peace by building on your relationship with Sinan. This seems like a unique opportunity for both of our peoples. But I leave the choice of whether you remain or not to you. Should you choose to accept this mission, Roland, the manner in which you proceed will be decided by your own judgment."

"Sire, I serve at your pleasure and will do my best to accomplish our goals."

Henry next summoned Pierre Duchien. Duchien wore the

black tunic with red cross and black mantle of a sergeant's rank. He was a man of common roots, practical and trustworthy, friendly with both Roland and Guillaume. Forty-two years old, Duchien was a dedicated warrior whose loyalty to the Templar Order had been tested and proven. He nodded in acknowledgment as he spoke to the king.

Roland walked over to Andre. They talked quietly, after which a reluctant Andre took leave of his friend.

"God protect you, Roland. Perhaps He has a purpose for you here."

"Indeed. Perhaps He does."

As the Crusaders rode off, Guillaume caught Pierre's eye. Roland's youth and inexperience made him a likely receptacle of the heresy and even idolatry to which he would surely be exposed by the Saracen enemy. Perhaps Pierre could offer some stability. At the very least he could provide accurate information to his wary commander. They nodded a mutual understanding of the dangers ahead as Guillaume rode out of the castle gates.

PART THREE

THE TEACHINGS OF SINAN

✠

CHAPTER 13

Sinan and Roland reclined on pillows conversing together in the room of leisure of the castle. A gentle breeze wafted through open curtains. Servants laid out a variety of refreshments and the two men were at their ease.

Sinan began what would become the first stage of Roland's education in esoteric doctrine. He communicated in the language of his student's culture.

"I am struck by the wisdom of your Bible. One passage seems particularly close to our own teaching. The prophet Jesus states, 'Let thine eye be single, and thy whole body shall be filled with light.' I am curious to know how you were taught to accomplish this."

Roland was utterly baffled by the question. Although he had often studied the New Testament, asking questions about textual subtleties was not a part of his Bible studies.

"I know the verse, but I never heard anyone say that it described a *practice*."

"Curious. I interpret those words as spoken by an adept deeply learned in the Wisdom Tradition."

Roland was even more taken aback.

"May I ask how you understand it?"

"We believe that deep within every man and every woman is a divine nature, and that one may attain awareness of this by turning the mind inward. When a person has achieved some mastery of the technique and his attention becomes single-pointed, the inner vision is flooded with light. Such a student transcends the physical world, and his true spiritual nature is revealed. Thus the statement by the Prophet Jesus confirmed to me the mystic Truth inherent in your religion."

Roland contemplated Sinan's strange words. He had never heard anything like this before in his life.

✛ ✛ ✛

When Roland returned to his room later that evening, he experimented with the technique Sinan shared with him after he had asked for more information. The teacher called the practice *meditation*.

Alone, seated in silence with his legs crossed, his back held straight, and his eyes closed, Roland was conscious of his breathing as Sinan had suggested. He tried to focus his attention on his mind's eye, the single eye or third eye to which, Sinan explained, Jesus so clearly referred.

In a not-so-unusual case of beginner's luck, Roland experienced some success with his first try at meditation. He perceived himself surrounded by scintillating, brilliant light that seemed to extend to infinity. He sensed a vast vista of radiant energy that encircled what he now believed to be his essence, and he was bathed in its vibratory pulsations. Roland felt a great sense of both empowerment and purification. He was overcome with gratitude and enthusiasm.

Despite the many events of this very long and eventful day, when Roland extinguished the candle and lay down closing his eyes, he drifted into a peaceful and deep sleep almost at once.

CHAPTER 14

Several days later Roland was seated on a balcony in the evening breeze practicing meditation. His eyes were closed and he exhibited a look of intense concentration. After his initial success, Roland was discovering a greater need for self-discipline. Aisha walked onto the balcony. Roland heard her, happy for the distraction. He opened his eyes.

Admonishing him, Aisha commanded, "You must not allow yourself to be interrupted when you practice."

Roland was again struck by her otherworldly beauty and the sublimity of her dark and graceful energy. His short stay at Al-Kaph had already begun to work its magic on him. The rigid and fearful young man was finding the girders, which had bound his soul, beginning to loosen. He started to flirt with this exotic woman, she who had shared his vulnerability and acted as a guide to him.

"Some distractions are more easily ignored than others."

Ignoring his playful comment, Aisha instructed him in the technique she herself had been practicing under the guidance of Sinan.

"Close your eyes. Relax your neck and shoulders. Straighten your back a little. Breathe gently and evenly. Observe the rhythm of your breath."

Roland complied.

"Now clear your mind. Bring your attention to the space just above and between your eyes. Let the eye of your mind—the single eye between your two eyes—gaze inward into your body. Do you not feel the vastness?"

With his eyes still closed, Roland innocently attempted to flirt again, "You're an excellent teacher. I think I need a teacher!"

Sternly she snapped, "Quiet!"

She paused. "I, too, am just a beginner."

Aisha softened her tone and continued, "The tedium we experience in the initial stages of meditation has been compared to licking a stone. Looking inward demands persistence and patience. These you must teach yourself."

CHAPTER 15

Roland was enthusiastic about his meditation progress. He felt himself beginning to develop a calmer manner. He also became aware of a growing breadth in his outlook, as if his mind were gaining access to aspects both of himself and the world of which he had not been previously conscious.

His thought process was growing to encompass a wider range of information, thus opening his perceptions and thoughts to a greater appreciation and understanding of some of the fallacies of his earlier experience.

His daily conversations with Sinan were further illuminating. Sinan challenged his assumptions about every aspect of his beliefs, asking Roland to explain his understanding of various fundamentals of Christian doctrine and questioning him about his answers in some detail.

Sinan also introduced Roland to insights into the Ismaili religion and some of the personages who had inspired generations of Ismaili believers. This allowed Roland to appreciate the universality of certain behaviors and ideals that resonated with the inmost hopes, expectations, and desires of people across all time and culture.

Mansur al-Hallaj was one such teaching example. Sinan explained that the celebrated martyr was accused of preaching the Ismaili heresy and of refusing to back down from his repeated ecstatic proclamations of mystic unity with the living God. Al-Hallaj was arrested, tortured, and slain by the Sunni religious authorities of Baghdad. But his spirit lived on in the example he provided to others.

Roland recognized that al-Hallaj's unfaltering courage in the midst of such violent persecution was similar to stories of heroes and saints of Christianity. The shared values of distant peoples transcended their differences.

✠ ✠ ✠

One evening Roland and Pierre Duchien were deep in conversation. Roland tried to express his excitement about some of these newfound discoveries.

"Sinan is introducing me to an unfamiliar world that seems to exist both inside of myself and throughout the world."

The passion of the convert, perhaps, led him to hope Pierre would understand and appreciate the new path he was exploring. But Pierre was a simple and unimaginative man, a plodder, whose duty was ever clear and present before him.

"Sir Roland, sometimes all is not what it seems. Be cautious."

"I believe I can trust what the scriptures call the 'still small voice.'"

As if his worst imaginings had just been confirmed, Pierre looked at his young charge with concern.

"Guillaume fears you could be the victim of witchcraft."

Roland was amused at the contrast between his commander's prejudices and the expansion of his self-awareness he was undergoing at Al-Kaph.

"Guillaume is ever filled with distrust."

CHAPTER 16

Within the castle was a secret Temple to which Roland had not yet been introduced. Aisha came by his quarters earlier in the day to tell him to prepare himself with meditation for a summons from Sinan. An hour later she came back to lead the young man toward the Temple.

The room was square, some 600 feet in area, with a high ceiling. Its walls were draped with exotic tapestries. A large candle stood at each of the four cardinal directions. A circle, some twelve feet in diameter, was painted on the floor. Just east of the center was a rectangular altar on which was placed an incense burner that filled the room with fragrant smoke.

Aisha and Roland entered, observing Sinan holding a magical wand and moving in a graceful yet highly energized spiral dance. He was swiftly whirling clockwise around the circle while turning upon his axis in a counterclockwise rotation. The room was filled with a palpable sense of power. Roland marveled at such grace, yet was gripped with a certain terror. Sinan's motions seemed to be creating an energy vortex the likes of which Roland had never experienced.

When Sinan reached the west of the Temple, he stood in place holding the upright wand against his chest and proclaimed in a dramatic voice, "Within me the Powers!"

Swirls of incense filled the air, revealing the same mysterious, semitransparent face in each of the four directions. It was golden in color with features indicating a bearded man whose piercing eyes riveted Roland to his soul, demanding the aspirant's full attention. Upon the face was superimposed a downward-pointing pentagram. The pentagram framed the head, its two upraised points suggesting horns, as if the figure was that of the Great God Pan.

"For about me flames my Father's face, the Star of Force and Fire!"

Sinan was standing in a column of Light that extended above and below him to Infinity. In both directions, as if forming a horizontal ceiling and floor, the face was again visible, this time with hexagrams superimposed upon it.

"And in the Column shines His six-rayed Splendor!"

Sinan finished the rite with a further series of gestures and movements, the intoning of certain mysterious Names, and stood before the altar in silence, breathing deeply.

He then walked calmly over to Roland and Aisha.

Roland felt his own senses attuned to the vibratory energy of the ritual. He exclaimed, "The room is tingling with power!"

Sinan nodded and explained, "It is a type of moving meditation. We imitate the motion of the stars, and thereby partake of their splendor."

He smiled at Roland with a quizzical and almost lighthearted look.

"Would you like to try it?"

Roland nodded and the three of them began to discuss the ritual while Sinan methodically demonstrated the choreography.

Roland began to learn the ritual and the dance in a private garden. As he practiced the spiral dance, he became dizzy, stumbling at first. Aisha hid nearby among the trees, watching him. She laughed to herself as she remembered her own efforts to master the whirling movements. Sinan walked up and stood beside her and watched. As the awkward Roland stumbled yet again, Sinan, too, smiled.

Roland was determined to master the rite and continued to work with the movements and improve his balance day after day. Sinan encouraged him to continue and helped guide him in his practice.

As Roland first stumbled and was dizzy, Sinan comforted him, "Dizziness and even nausea are common when first learning the dance. The body must be conquered and the dizziness overcome."

As Roland gained skill and found his point of balance while whirling and spinning, Sinan encouraged him to continue. After the first week of practice, Roland began to move with more grace. Later still, he was able to add more force to his movements.

It was then that Sinan explained the purpose of the motions, "The real power comes when you are able to rise beyond the physical body into the realm of spirit."

Finally, Roland moved without a trace of dizziness or hesitation. Sinan was delighted by his chela's progress. Roland had attained physical command of the dance.

"Now you can start to experience true oneness with the Divine. The dance takes us beyond ourselves. The dancer becomes the dance. Overcoming the limitations of the body begins to reveal your stellar nature, your identity with the cosmos."

Finally, tingling with power, Roland proclaimed, "Within me the Powers!"

CHAPTER 17

Some weeks later, Roland and Pierre were walking and talking together in the courtyard. The early evening stars were bright as the moon climbed higher in the sky. Pierre was troubled and openly expressed his fears to Roland.

"But my lord. You spend so much time with him."

"Pierre, remember that King Henry tasked me with understanding these people. And the exercises Sinan has taught me have awakened me to a new sense of myself."

Pierre's concerns were rooted in the medieval fear of the Devil. He warned his hierarchical superior of his doubts.

"Do we Christians not believe that the Devil is a tempter—that he may appear in the guise of a friend or mentor to mislead us?"

"That has been my fear too, Pierre. But God has also given us the ability to know His Truth. I feel I am on the right path."

With anxiety evident in his tone, Pierre replied, "I hope so, sir."

Later that night, Roland was alone in his room. He knelt in prayer.

"Lord, I am in a strange new world. Familiar voices that seem to come from my childhood warn me that I am surrounded by heathens, that my soul may be in mortal danger. Yet I feel closer to You than ever before. I ask for Your guidance."

He crossed himself. He tried to summon the reverence he knew should accompany this gesture but was acutely aware of how distant and mechanical it now seemed.

Roland had been raised in a traditional Catholic family and community. His childhood education involved religious studies mixed with the more secular curriculum available to one of his social and economic class. Its subjects included language, mathematics, science, and some literature. Yet, all his courses referred back to the Bible since his tutors were always monks. Prayer was as much a part of his training as any other subject.

He lay awake for a time, trying to understand what was happening to him.

CHAPTER 18

Sinan and Roland walked along the battlements of Al-Kaph in the cool of the night, conversing under a sky brilliant with stars.

"What I've learned during these months has opened a whole new world to me. I never thought that mere human beings could experience such things!"

Sinan jumped on Roland's words. While he had not objected to Roland's dismissive use of the phrase "mere human beings" before his formal training began, Sinan knew it was time for Roland to understand that he was unwittingly expressing the key error of Christian thought. Sinan was about to reveal the crux of the Gnostic doctrine.

"Never say mere! Human beings are never mere."

He paused and went on, "The Christians speak of the depravity of man and of his evil and sinful heart."

Sinan shook his head and looked up at the firmament.

"We are not base beings. The human spirit is divine. Every man and every woman is a star!"

After a time they resumed walking, each silently musing upon his own thoughts.

"Your progress here has been swift, Roland. Through meditation, you are beginning to tame and focus the mind. Through the whirling dance of the heavens, you have enlisted the aid of the body. But there is more to learn.

"There are sources of power of which you still remain ignorant. The ascent through the spheres is greatly facilitated by the sensual faculties. It now becomes part of your training to enlist the passions—the sacred union of opposing energies— to continue the Great Work of discovering and cultivating the deity within."

Roland replied uneasily, "If by 'the passions' you mean . . . well, I . . . as a Templar, I have taken certain vows . . ."

Sinan nodded in understanding.

"And is the misguided oath of the child to forever burden the man?"

Looking at Roland, he continued, "Magic involves raising energy and directing it toward a goal. There are many ways to raise magical energy. Harnessing the power created during the sexual union of male and female is one of the most effective.

"While locked in harmonious embrace, one learns to perceive one's partner as a channel for, and vehicle of, the divine. The bonding of male and female is a shadow of the cosmic act of creation itself. The accompanying state of bliss is a mirror of the ecstasy of union with the most sacred energies of the universe.

"You have worked hard to reach your current state. You must not hesitate to open the next door."

CHAPTER 19

Aisha's nakedness seemed to fill the room with its radiance as the candlelight played off her skin. She lowered herself into her bath, its waters rendered silken smooth by the oils poured by her attendants.

Her characteristic intensity was softened by the leisurely ablution, yet it was also clear that she was deeply focused in concentration.

She rose in her splendor and was wrapped in a luxurious towel, then dried and perfumed. She was clothed in a gossamer ruby gown whose color perfectly highlighted her own rich tones.

Roland was in another chamber being ritually bathed by female servants. The depth of the conflicts and shyness he felt at first was gradually giving way to the relaxation he was able to attain through his meditation and the warmth of the water. The unfamiliar presence of the women became less intimidating as he sought deep within himself for equilibrium. He worked to suspend judgment through an act of will. His trust in Sinan and his attraction to Aisha had, for now, overcome the internal voices of his conditioning.

He was then clothed in a blue robe and led into a magnificent chamber. Like the private Temple, this room was draped in sensuous fabrics and gently lit by candles in the four quarters. A magnificent bed commanded the center of the space. The servants turned down the covers and left him alone.

Aisha entered the chamber in her ruby gown. A pearl necklace dramatically complemented her skin. She smiled at the young knight.

Her voice, rich in a sultry softness that Roland had never heard her—or any woman—use before, intoned the words of a secret sacred text.

"Come forth, O children, under the stars, and take your fill of love."

Roland looked deeply into her eyes. He reached out his hand to touch her neck, the first time he had touched a woman with intimacy. Her hand caressed his face.

She allowed her robe to open, revealing her nakedness. The sight took his breath away. Roland experienced an erotic longing that was entirely free and unfettered from the restrictions of a lifetime of repression.

Aisha let the robe fall from her shoulders and stood before him. She beckoned him to approach closer and opened his robe. She touched him. Their bodies came together in a sensuous embrace as she whispered the immortal promise of the Goddess to Her devotees.

"I give unimaginable joys on earth."

They moved to the bed. Roland's passion blazed like a fire as he sought to maintain the single-pointed focus of his will.

The skilled Initiatrix worked her magic on her partner as she entwined her limbs around him, drawing him into her. Their bodies became as one, moving together in a slow and intimate rhythm.

Roland's inner vision was opened to a scene of infinite proportion. The space around him and his consort was filled with a light that grew brighter as they maintained their embrace. He perceived himself and Aisha assuming an archetypal magnitude, expanding to encompass all of creation, as if they had become the primeval generators of universal form.

As they continued their lovemaking, Roland was aware of the room itself becoming suffused with an electric, pulsating energy. Patterns of colored light sparkled before, around, and within them, brilliantly illuminating the candlelit chamber.

Aisha again intoned the words of the ancient scripture.

"I am uplifted in thine heart, and the kisses of the stars rain hard upon thy body!"

The sensuous interplay of the act of love, the conjoining of their earthly vehicles, had drawn back the veil on their cosmic identity.

As they reached the climax of their passion, they lost their physical forms entirely, moving beyond the ecstasy of the senses to the ecstasy of the divine. They were transformed—at first into individual energy patterns, then blending together in an explosive burst of light and color in which all was dissolved.

CHAPTER 20

Roland wrestled for some days afterward with a mix of contradictory emotions. So steeped was he since childhood in the doctrine of the Devil—and under the strict vows of the monastic Order to which he had pledged his life—doubts about his experience with Aisha were to be expected. But these were offset by a sense of the rightness of their actions together and the knowledge that he was growing beyond anything he had ever imagined himself to become.

Late one evening, he walked into Pierre's room as Pierre was preparing for bed. He hesitated.

"Pierre, please forgive my intrusion. May we speak?"

Pierre rose from his pallet. "But of course, my lord."

"I am confused. I feel I no longer understand the true nature of sin. And I don't know why I don't know. We have been taught the nature of sin since we were children."

Pierre was happy to hear Roland express such uncertainty and truth seeking. His greatest fear had been that Roland was blindly plunging ahead into this strange new world of the Infidel with no hesitation or awareness of the spiritual dangers threatening him at every turn. The fact that he now seemed troubled and in doubt reassured Pierre. He brought forth his own doctrinal certainty with firm resolve.

"The teachings of the Church and our Order are so clear about this matter of sin."

"I know. But it seems to me that sin should *feel* wrong if it is truly evil. Has not God given us our hearts to know right from wrong?"

"Man is born into sin. How can you—a mere man—trust your heart?"

Pierre's words caused Roland to nod in thought. He finally understood the nature of his dilemma.

"A 'mere man,' indeed. Thank you, Pierre."

✛ ✛ ✛

Roland walked out of the room with a growing understanding of the distance between himself and his past. The clarity about the depth of his estrangement from the faith and beliefs of his entire life prior to Al-Kaph was, in one sense, reassuring. While he anticipated that his journey would be fraught with further challenges, he knew he had truly moved beyond his old ways. There was no turning back. A "mere man" indeed.

CHAPTER 21

Roland's next challenge to the totality of his former self came even sooner than he anticipated. Summoned by a servant to join Sinan in the private Temple, Roland entered alone.

Sinan stood before the altar. A beautifully fashioned Golden Head rested upon a ruby-colored plate arranged in the center of the altar top. Black cords were laid around the plate and surrounded the head.

As Roland approached Sinan at the altar, he gazed upon this strange and otherworldly tableau with a combination of curiosity, fear, and awe.

Sinan explained, "This is a likeness of my Brother and Master Hasan *ala dhikrhi as salam*. Those words mean, 'upon whose mention be peace.' A skilled artisan made a death mask of his face. It was later used to fashion this Golden Head, a symbol of our source of wisdom.

Sinan continued, "In our language, we call it *Abufihamet*— 'father of understanding.'"

Roland was startled. Mispronouncing the name, he exclaimed, "This *Baphomet* . . . I recognize it! It is the face I saw as you performed your dance! And I have seen it in my own practice as well. What does it mean?"

"This is the face of one who has come to enlightenment. One who has successfully transmuted his consciousness through the practices you have been studying. A man who experienced union with the divine and pointed the way for others to do the same. He was my friend and teacher. And he died for his Truth."

In his mind's eye Sinan traveled back nearly four decades to 1166. It was two years after Hasan's Qiyama ceremony. Sinan was celebrating his own Qiyama rite here at Al-Kaph. He was unaware of a dark scene taking place almost nine hundred miles away at Alamut.

His beloved Teacher, Hasan II, was seated in deep meditation. The anti-Qiyama faction at Alamut had been continuously plotting to end the apostasy of their leader by any means necessary. They were as fervent in their religious orthodoxy as Hasan was confident in the creative power of his revelation.

A raging Assassin—Hasan's own brother-in-law—burst through the door of the meditation chamber with dagger in hand screaming in fury.

"You have violated the teachings of the Prophet! You have insulted Allah. You have dishonored Alamut. I slay you in the Name of Islam! *Allahu Akbar!*"

Hasan continued to gaze into Eternity as the dagger plunged into his back. His clean white robe was stained red with blood.

Sinan returned his consciousness to the present and, utterly focused, began the ceremony of Roland's initiation. Roland stood before the altar.

"You will now remove your robe."

Roland was surprised by this request, but complied and stood naked before him. Sinan took one of the black cords from the ruby plate.

"I tie this cord around your waist as a symbol of your intention to perform the Great Work. The Great Work means that you pledge to discover and accomplish the true purpose of your life.

"This cord shall ever remind you that you have bound yourself to Truth, and that Truth shall be your strength. This cord shall also remind you of the unbreakable bond between you and me. You will never remove it as long as you live."

He paused to allow the import of his words to penetrate Roland's psyche.

"I now clothe you in the white robe of our Order."

Sinan slipped a bright new robe over Roland's head as the candidate extended his arms to enter the sleeves.

Roland gazed at Sinan with a look of love and pride.

CHAPTER 22

The next day, Roland and Sinan were walking together in the private garden enjoying a late morning conversation. Sinan unrolled a parchment.

"I have received a letter from King Henry requesting your temporary return to Acre. The Templars have been called to defend the coastal fortresses. There is a shortage of experienced knights to protect the pilgrim routes to Galilee. You are needed to help organize and command the patrols.

"I suspect, however, that there is a deeper motive in recalling you—to discuss your dispatches and to candidly assess my strength and intentions."

Roland replied, "That is probable."

Sinan continued, "I will inform Henry of your imminent departure—and reemphasize the importance I attach to your return. Henry is well aware that his position against both Cairo and Damascus is strengthened by his continued friendship with me. He will not deny me.

"Your return to Acre also represents an opportunity for us. The time has come for you to advance the spiritual understanding of your own people. You have spoken of your desire to share what you've learned and your hope that some of your brothers may be receptive to our teaching."

Roland pictured the Templar fortress and imagined the men drilling in the courtyard. He expected that his friend Andre would be commanding the group. Roland knew that Andre had both the requisite trust in Roland and the spiritual hunger to seek and to learn.

"My friend and fellow Templar, Andre, is the best candidate. Since childhood we have spoken of God, the Church, and our most personal doubts and questions about these matters. He is honorable and trustworthy, and a seeker of Truth."

"Then begin with him."

✛ ✛ ✛

Pierre Duchien was saddling up in the courtyard. He was joined by a young fidai named Ahmed who had been assigned by Sinan as a guide and bodyguard to accompany Roland and Pierre on their journey to Acre. Roland, dressed in full armor and his Templar regalia, led his own horse into the courtyard and joined them. Sinan approached.

"Travel safely, my son. I look forward to your return when the moon has completed her six revolutions. Be watchful. Eyes filled with distrust will follow you. Your long stay here makes you a target of small and suspicious minds."

"I will be vigilant, my lord."

Roland gazed up at the balcony where Aisha was looking on with affection. He then mounted up, saluted Sinan, and set out with Pierre and Ahmed toward Acre.

PART FOUR

THE GNOSIS SPREADS WEST

CHAPTER 23

The three travelers rode through the Syrian mountains and then along the Mediterranean coast for the 150 miles of their journey. After a week's ride, they arrived safely before the walls of the Templar headquarters. Ahmed was fed and his horse watered by stable hands. He paid his respects to Roland and Pierre and began the trip back to Al-Kaph.

Roland entered the Templar barracks and found his own small monastic cell. The room contained a straw mattress with a writing table and chair. A crucifix hung prominently on one wall. He looked at the image of the dead body of Jesus on the cross with a certain air of bewilderment.

As he removed his mantle and armor, he was shaken from his reverie by Andre's enthusiastic entrance.

"Roland! Finally!"

They were delighted to see each other after their long period of separation. They embraced as brothers.

"Are you back for good?"

"Six months, Andre. How are you?"

"Things have been fairly quiet—at least here. Sinan's alliance with Henry helps keep the peace."

Andre could barely contain his happiness and his curiosity.

"Tell me about Sinan! You must have gotten to know him well over this past year and a half."

Roland replied thoughtfully, "Sinan is a remarkable man, Andre, a man of wisdom and honor; he has become like a father to me."

Andre reacted with surprise at the depth of Roland's unexpected fondness for the Assassin king.

Roland continued, "You and I have a lot to talk about."

"It will have to wait. Our illustrious commander Guillaume de Gonneville requests the honor of your presence in his office—now!"

Both men laughed as Roland reached again for his mantle.

CHAPTER 24

Roland approached the door of Guillaume's office and knocked.

"Enter."

Guillaume was sitting at his desk and writing, seemingly ignoring Roland's entrance.

Roland stood before the commander's desk and waited. Finally, Guillaume looked up and spoke in a voice filled with sarcasm.

"The prodigal returns . . . but not for long, or so I've been told."

After a pause, he continued. "I've read your dispatches, and I must say that I'm disturbed by their tone. I fear you are no longer seeing things clearly."

"Sir, if I may . . ."

"You may *not!*"

For a tense moment, they looked appraisingly at each other. Guillaume then appeared to soften his gaze and assume a more paternalistic tone.

"It's only natural, when living among any people—even an uncivilized and barbaric people—to develop a degree of sympathy for them—to overlook their faults and shortcomings. But you must remember that, in the end, there can only be hostility between Christian and Infidel.

"Yes, we have treaties with certain Saracen leaders. We're practical men after all. But such treaties are for our convenience. We do not fraternize with the enemy. Nor are we the least bit curious about their heathen religion. I hope that is clear."

"It is, sir."

"Good. Now that you're here and can speak frankly, you will convey—in detail—your true assessment of what you observed at Al-Kaph."

"Sir, my reports have been quite candid, I assure you. I was under no coercion."

"You *were*, whether you realized it or not. You're on patrol tonight. I'll expect your revised report in three days' time."

He turned back to his paperwork.

"Dismissed!"

After Roland left the office, Pierre Duchien entered.

Guillaume uncharacteristically expressed his concern. He knew that he and Pierre shared the same sense that Roland was in danger. Roland's youth and immaturity made him a target.

"I am worried about Roland."

"As am I, sir. He seems to grow ever closer to the Infidel."

"I know that King Henry expects you both to return to Al-Kaph before very long. Pierre, you must remain ever watchful for Roland's soul."

Guillaune knew that Pierre did not suffer from the complex inner fires that raged inside him. Guillaume was a man who fought a constant battle between the power of his instinctual drives and the internal rigidity of his own psyche. He was also prone to imaginative flights of fancy and fought such creative indulgences with all his conscious will. He therefore had a certain awareness of the subtlety of the challenges facing Roland. Guillaume understood that Pierre was a more simple-minded soul—that he would remain immune to the temptations of the heresy surrounding Roland. Pierre could be trusted to perform his duty, to observe and report objectively without hesitation or self-doubt.

CHAPTER 25

In the countryside that night, Andre and Roland were sitting by a campfire. Roland stirred a cauldron. Other soldiers were busy elsewhere with various tasks.

Roland began to share his feelings with his friend. The reflectiveness of his tone was balanced by his happiness at their ability to communicate openly and honestly. They had been friends their entire lives. Their parents' estates in Avignon abutted each other. They had spent much time as children playing hide-and-seek around the barns and fields of their farms, swimming in streams and fighting mock battles with wooden swords. As they grew older, they rode horses through the woods and valleys, imagining themselves as knights in armor. They hunted the plentiful small game in the region and spent many nights camped out under the stars, deep in the conversations of youth. Roland was now most grateful for their long familiarity after so long a time in the company of people with whom he had no shared memories.

"Andre, I have tread upon a path that some would call evil, others heretical. Yet, I feel I am approaching Truth."

"You and I have long searched together for our true purpose, never satisfied with what others tell us. What have you discovered?"

"During my stay with Sinan, I learned that God is within me, and so is Heaven. I have learned to close my eyes and find both."

"You seem so sure of yourself, so certain your thoughts are real."

"Indeed. But I have had to work long and hard for the insights I have gained. It has not come without cost."

"What do you mean by that?"

Roland grew more serious and lowered his tone.

"I find myself moving further from the religion of my birth. A power grows in me that challenges everything I have ever been taught."

"Fascinating. But why does that trouble you so?"

Solemnly Roland replied, "Because if I am wrong, I know my soul shall be condemned to the fires of Hell."

"That *is* a heavy burden."

"It is terrible and frightening. But I have never felt so exhilarated. I no longer seek to be counted among the meek and poor-in-spirit. I feel a pride that once I might have called satanic, but which I now accept as the proper condition of an awakened individual. I have come to judge right and wrong for myself."

"The promise of inner power excites me—as you knew it would."

"Yes I did, old friend."

"Will you share it with me?"

"Happily," Roland replied. "Have we not always shared?"

Over the following weeks, Andre took every opportunity to work on the meditation practices Roland taught him, sometimes with and sometimes without Roland's presence.

As they were cleaning their armor and weapons in the armory one evening, they were alone and able to converse quietly. Andre was enthusiastic and shared his progress.

"How simple—yet profound! I find myself aware of my own mind! I feel an energy inside me, as if a serpent is awakening and about to shoot up my spine!"

"It's just the beginning, Andre. Later, you'll start counting your breaths, repeating sacred words, and learning to concentrate on chosen thoughts and images. The effect is incredible! It will change you in ways you cannot guess."

Andre nodded as Roland continued.

"Behind the everyday world lies another world, a spiritual

world of knowledge and power. We can use it to grow—to become more than we are now—stronger, wiser, better able to help others."

There followed a long pause as Andre's demeanor changed from enthusiasm to concern.

"Roland, I know a young brother named Landro de Villiers. He is deeply troubled by many of the same questions you and I have discussed. He's spoken to me of his doubts and feelings of separation from God and the Church. He was choked with emotion."

Roland pondered this information for a time. He did not know Landro, a recent European arrival. But he sensed the potential of pursuing his mission among more of his Templar brothers. He spoke up.

"We must find the means to safely open a conversation about such things with others—a strategy to protect ourselves from the unworthy, who might take it the wrong way and cause us trouble.

"Guillaume is already suspicious of me due to the time I've spent with Sinan. Yet I'm charged with spreading the Gnosis to those who search with pure hearts."

Andre had never heard the term "Gnosis" and asked Roland to explain.

"Gnosis means 'knowledge.' People who seek the direct experience of God within the body are called Gnostics. Can you arrange for Landro to join us on patrol?"

CHAPTER 26

Sometime after this conversation the three Templars were riding in the countryside together, along with a small squadron of a dozen knights and sergeants. Roland, Andre, and Landro rode at the head of the column. Landro was younger than his companions, twenty years old and slightly built.

A horseman galloped up toward the group frantically waving his arm.

"Saracens are moving in force less than a league to the east! They mean to ambush the pilgrim caravan traveling to Nazareth!"

Roland rallied the men, "Ahead—full gallop!"

Riding like lightning they reached the top of a hill. From this vantage point, they could see the Saracen raiders already attacking the pilgrim convoy.

Roland drew his sword and commanded the squadron.

"Prepare to engage!"

Surveying the readiness of his men and the action below, he bellowed, "Charge!"

The Templars rode at a full gallop, their mantles flying in the wind, swords pointed forward, the steel of their helmets flashing in the sun. They were outnumbered, yet engaged the Saracen raiders without fear or hesitation.

During the fighting, Roland was unhorsed and set upon by a half dozen of the enemy, both on foot and on horseback.

In an astounding display of martial arts and magical prowess, Roland took them all on simultaneously. Adapting the movements of the spiral dance to this combat encounter, Roland's sword became an extension of his outstretched arm. He spun upon his axis counterclockwise, forming an impenetrable defensive shield of flashing steel. As he whirled clockwise in a circle, he continued to widen his area of domination over his opponents. The enhanced energy he had mastered made Roland appear at times to be almost flying. Finally, the six Saracen warriors lay dead at his feet.

When the fight was over, Andre and Landro stared at Roland in open-mouthed amazement. Never had either of them witnessed such an incredible exhibition.

Later that evening, as the sun began to set, the three Templars were standing on a hill, looking down into the valley. All were silent as they gazed toward the horizon. Finally, Andre asked Roland to explain.

"Do you want to talk about what we saw today?"

Roland hesitated for a moment. He looked at Landro with some tenderness and the awareness that he was about to reveal a dangerous truth about himself to a relative stranger. But he trusted Andre's assessment of the young man so proceeded.

"Sinan taught me that true magic means attaining higher levels of wisdom and self-knowledge. But magical practices can result in other abilities as well. As we come to know the divine force, we learn to align ourselves with it and draw upon that energy."

Andre quipped, "And to perform feats of great skill and agility, apparently!"

Landro was aware that the two friends had accepted him into their confidence and spoke up humbly.

"The extraordinary stories we've heard about the Old Man of the Mountain—are they really true?"

"I've seen him penetrate into the deepest recesses of a man's heart as if he were reading a book. I've seen him cause the earth to quake. I've talked with people who watched him stop the approach of a hostile army by immobilizing the soldiers as if they were statues. Whether this was his power or God's, I cannot say. Perhaps there is no difference."

Landro replied, "How do you square such things with our

faith? Some would call it the work of the Devil. Yet I sense that this is more than just heathen magic."

Roland answered honestly. "This question has been my greatest challenge. All my life, I believed that God's will is revealed in the Scriptures and the Church. I was born into that belief, never challenging it. But now I have learned to seek for God within myself."

Roland's voice trailed off. The three men stood in silence, looking into the glow of a particularly fiery sunset.

Roland spoke up again with passionate intensity befitting the evening splendor.

"Can such a quest be wrong if God has placed it within my grasp? Can the powers he has opened be the illusions of the Devil? It does not *feel* like that to me."

Landro, in despair, replied, "The horrors I've seen in this land have made me doubt that God even exists."

"Perhaps God uses our doubts to invite us to know Him better."

"How does one come to know God?"

"In silence, my friend, in silence. If you will pledge your silence, I will gladly share what I have learned. A gift so precious can only be retained by sharing it with others."

Roland clasped Landro's shoulder.

"Landro, my young brother, if you choose to explore this path, we have much to do. I have but a short time left here. We will need to take every opportunity to talk—night watches, patrols, our daily chores. Then you and Andre will pursue your efforts together until I return again from Al-Kaph."

After a moment, he added.

"I, too, have more to learn."

CHAPTER 27

Soon after, alone in his cell one night, Roland tossed and turned in his bed, finally rising and assuming a meditation posture.

He prayed, "Lord, I now reach out to others in your Name. I am a warrior, with blood on my hands. Cleanse my heart that I may be a fit vessel of Thy Truth."

Several days later Roland was riding alone through the streets of Acre. He was attracted by a small Catholic church along the way and stopped. Tying his horse to a post, he walked in. He looked around cautiously, then entered a confessional.

He began his confession with this statement.

"Father, forgive me, for I no longer seek salvation from sin—but from ignorance."

The priest, a man in his early seventies, was startled. Sitting behind the screen of the confessional, he had to admit to himself that he was intrigued by this unexpected statement.

Then he spoke aloud to Roland. "Freeing oneself from ignorance is a worthy endeavor, my son. Knowledge is a virtue. But to ignore sin is a grave error."

"But Father, I no longer see sin where I once saw it."

"Sin is sin, my son. Sin separates us from God."

"Separated from God? Father, some believe that human and divine are one—that man is a divine being in a physical body."

The priest replied, "The prophet Jeremiah tells us that 'the heart is deceitful above all things, and desperately wicked.' Only by divine grace can we be rescued from our evil natures."

"Is evil then our true spiritual nature? And who was Jeremiah that I should believe him?"

"It is a sin to question the Holy Scriptures, my son."

"Father, all my life I have believed in the Scriptures. But now, so much does not ring true. I've looked inside myself and seen light, not wickedness. And I have seen the same light in others. Would God have me reject my own experience?"

"Your conviction is strong—unusual in one so young."

"Father, I have walked in the Light, a light that is brilliant and true and good and beautiful! I have seen visions. I have talked with angels. My doubts about God have vanished like mist before the rays of the sun. I know that God is within me—that I am a part of God, and God is a part of me. And before that knowledge I bow in awe and wonder!"

The priest said nothing, lost in his own reflections.

Roland continued, "Does God require me to abandon that which has made me whole, has made me a better man? Am I to return to the darkness and ignorance of my past, to a Church that tells me I am sinful and depraved and worthless, to a belief that crushes my passion for living?"

The priest replied with anger, "For such words, I should command you to throw yourself before the cross and beg for your eternal life!"

He then let out a long sigh.

"But I will not. If what you say is true, you have touched the highest things that are given a man to see and to know. Can that which enlightens the mind and comforts the heart be the Devil's work?"

He paused again thoughtfully, impressed and troubled by this young warrior.

"If God has made Himself known within you, who am I to deny it? Did not our Lord say to the Jews, 'Is it not written in your law, "I said, you are gods"?'"

Roland and the priest sat in silence.

"The divine within you has spoken to me today, Father. Thank you."

The priest answered him in a whisper, "And to me, my son, and to me."

PART FIVE

RETURN TO AL-KAPH
AND DEATH

✠

CHAPTER 28

The time for Roland to depart Acre had come. He was confident that Andre and Landro were both making progress and that the bonds between the three of them were firmly established. He looked forward to returning to Al-Kaph to continue his own work. Ahmed had arrived to accompany him and Pierre on their return journey, and the three men rode together on the now-familiar coastal journey through Israel and Syria until they entered the foothills of the Nusayri Mountains.

Roland was happy to be back at the Assassin headquarters, an environment he had come to consider as much a home as his native France. He found Sinan reading a scroll in the library. Sinan laid the document aside and rose to greet him with tenderness.

"Welcome back, my son! How was your stay at Acre?"

"All is well. I have opened the teachings to my friend Andre. Another Templar brother has joined us as well."

"Excellent!"

He then asked with a smile, "And how did you fare with your commander?"

Roland laughed. "Not quite as well. He is much opposed to King Henry's friendship with you—and very hostile to my continued presence here. Only his fear of Henry and my father's influence prevents him from pressing the issue."

"I believe he has now fully enlisted your servant Pierre as his personal spy. However, it is our task to proceed with the Great Work. We will do our part by remaining conscious of the challenge. The future will fulfill itself."

Sinan paused and continued.

"You have returned at an opportune moment."

CHAPTER 29

Sometime later, Roland found himself in the Temple with Sinan. The room had been entirely draped in rich blue curtains. Cedar incense wafted toward the ceiling. Four blue candles were arranged in the north, south, east, and west.

A new altar stood in the center of the circle. Gold and sapphires were arranged upon it in the shape of a square. In the middle rested a large, highly polished tin statue of a great king, reminiscent of the Greek god Zeus. A pyramid-shaped amethyst was displayed prominently in front of the deity.

Sinan stood before the altar wearing a crown of gold and a blue velvet robe. In his right hand he held a scepter. Roland was draped in a rough rustic cloak. He was holding a shepherd's crook and standing to the right of and just behind Sinan.

This was the climax of a long and energetic invocation.

Sinan's voice echoed through the room with a power that Roland had never heard from the Mystic.

"O Thou mighty and beneficent King, whose Joy is in the well-being and prosperity of Thy realm, fill us with Thy presence. Imbue us with Thy power! Appear Thou glorious before us!"

The smoke of the incense seemed to come alive. Sinan raised the wand high above his head and continued in an even louder and more sonorous voice, his entire being resonating with an ecstatic power.

"I am Thou! It is I who tread upon the Firmament!"

Sinan seemed to grow to a vast height as the Temple dissolved and the scene became that of Galactic Space. His scepter glowed with energy and began to emit streams of light.

"I wield the scepter of Amun!"

The scintillating light spread forth from the wand in all directions, filling the room with a sparkling energy. Roland was poised in an altered state of awareness—a kind of ecstasy laced with a sense of awe, suspended between the feeling of overwhelming power and a dizziness that might have caused him to faint. The visions arising in his mind replaced any sensory input. He had fully entered astral consciousness.

Roland watched as the Earth came into view as if from space. The level of power in the room grew to an almost unbearable crescendo as Sinan's voice resounded with ever-increasing volume.

"I fill the land with Glory! Mine is the fountain of wealth and good fortune! It is I who flood the world with joy!"

Roland now perceived the Temple as being filled with whirling discrete energy patterns suggesting the spirits of the four Elements. The Water spirits were a rich blue; the Air spirits shimmered in silver; the Fire spirits flamed in red; the Earth spirits were of a greenish brown. Although faceless and indistinct, they all seemed to move at Sinan's command.

Sinan proclaimed, "I control every spirit of the Firmament and of the Aethyr. All spirits upon the Earth, and in the Water, of whirling Air, and rushing Fire answer to my command. Every Spell and Scourge of God is obedient unto Me!"

Sinan had reached the climax of the rite. Roland perceived the image of his Master's body becoming enveloped by an even greater image of the god Jupiter. Sinan fully merged and united with the deity as Roland's cognitive mind was simply displaced by the direct communication with his unconscious self.

Roland saw Sinan/Jupiter with a long white beard and long white hair. His skin tone was now of a golden hue. He was cloaked in blue, holding an even larger scepter. Roland became aware that Sinan's eyes were looking forth from the eyes of that higher being. Simultaneously Roland was able to see the physical face of Sinan radiating with an expression of ecstatic union with Jupiter.

Sinan had *become* Jupiter/Amun. He wielded all the power and understanding of that eternal cosmic archetype. His sonorous voice proclaimed the identification in no uncertain terms. Roland felt buffeted about by a power beyond his comprehension.

"For I am Jupiter-Amun! I am He who doth administer His kingdom with Mercy, and from whose mighty hands issue forth the bounteous fullness of the Lord to his people!"

The room filled with a fluorescent, bluish radiance. Sinan was immersed in a visible energy field; he glowed with its brilliance, his body pulsating with power.

Roland was at last overcome by the intensity of the blinding luminescence. He lowered himself slowly to the floor and sat, lest he should lose his balance and fall.

CHAPTER 30

Roland became aware that he and Sinan had moved into the room of leisure. Roland lay on a pillow, disoriented. Aisha entered his awareness. She brought him a welcomed goblet of water.

He saw Sinan seated upon a pillow in meditation. The Master was wearing a turban with a large diamond in its center.

Roland asked in an incredulous voice, "What was that?"

Aisha smiled and replied in a gentle tone, "You met the god whom the Romans call Jupiter, the Greeks Zeus, the Egyptians Amun. You aren't used to direct contact with such powerful energies."

Sinan opened his eyes and spoke, "It was necessary that you experience the strength of invocation, that you doubt it not. Forces and energies exist within us and all around us.

"Through the assistance of a ritual such as this, it is possible to align oneself with a particular type of energy—deliberately call it forth—draw upon its strength.

"Today we invoked the god Jupiter. He provides the perfect model for someone with responsibilities such as my own. Like him, I am charged with the rulership of a vast people."

Sinan stood up and addressed the still-seated Roland.

"In the ritual, I began by preparing myself to become one with him. I proclaimed his powers and my intention to unite with them. I visualized and assumed his form by imitating his postures, gestures, clothing, and other attributes. I surrounded myself with the sights, sounds, and aromas that suggest him, including your own presence in the garb of his shepherd companion. I fully immersed myself in his qualities."

Sinan continued.

"As his energies built up inside me through the power of the ceremony, I actually became Jupiter! I united myself with his power and gained insights and strength to serve as a better leader to my people."

Roland was shaking his head in disbelief. He felt as if his mind was being strained beyond its capacity to accept new information.

"I am confused! We have discussed the oneness and identity of the Christian God and the Muslim Allah. You have shown me that they two are actually one—different names for the same Being. But now you add a new god? I just don't understand."

Sinan nodded in acknowledgment. This young Crusader was a brave and perceptive student. Sinan appreciated the honesty and integrity at the root of Roland's dilemma.

"I am reminded of the beautiful verse of the Jewish people: 'Hear O Israel, the Lord thy God, the Lord is One.' Those words are true. We Muslims say, 'there is no god but God.' There is but one secret and ineffable Lord—one omnipotent Creator of whose fire we are created, the source of all existence."

Sinan then removed the large diamond from his turban. As he moved it in his fingers, the light was reflected from its facets, radiating in all directions and throwing a rainbow of colors on the walls.

"This stone is one stone."

Sinan looked deeply into Roland's eyes.

"But divinity, like this diamond, is multi-faceted."

He went on patiently as he moved the diamond in his hand and the sunlight projected a rainbow kaleidoscope.

"See the light reflecting from its different facets. All of the gods and goddesses who have been worshipped through history are but different aspects or manifestations of the one divine being—divided for love's sake, for the chance of union.

"Each of the gods—each of the many faces of the One God—has a different attribute. Jupiter shows us God's quality of leadership and benevolence; Venus, God's love; Minerva, God's wisdom; Mars, God's strength. Those qualities can be brought directly into yourself as you saw today."

Aisha now spoke up, drawing Roland's attention to another mystery.

"Notice, too, the white light of the sun striking the stone. The stone breaks the light into many colors on the wall—red, yellow, blue. White light contains all colors."

Sinan continued with a beneficent look in his sparkling eyes.

"Many colors, yet the light is one. So it is with God."

CHAPTER 31

Later that night, Pierre Duchien was in his room, feverishly and furtively packing his gear and checking supplies. He was determined to escape Al-Kaph and return to Acre. He was increasingly troubled by his intuitive certainty that Roland's growing apostasy was moving beyond his control. Pierre concluded the situation was so dire his only hope of fulfilling the duty with which he had been charged by King Henry and Guillaume was to alert them to his overwhelming suspicions and encourage them to act before it was too late. What that action should be, the simple Pierre had no idea. But he knew that here was heresy, and he knew he must sound the alarm.

As he packed, an Assassin spy observed him. When Pierre left the castle, the fidai followed him.

Upon arising the next morning, Roland was called into the room of leisure where he found Sinan.

"Your servant Pierre was found fleeing to Acre to betray you. He is dead."

Roland was stunned. He exclaimed in horror, "But he was my brother!"

Sinan was firm.

"This is not a road for fools or weaklings. He intended to betray you, Roland. You must understand your choices and accept your responsibility."

Roland left Sinan and returned to his quarters. He lay on his bed, racked with anguish. He was aware that he had breached a fundamental barrier separating European Christianity and the Templars from the Assassins. Any acquiescence in Pierre's killing would be a clear case of moral and political treason. While he had certainly not taken Pierre's life with his own hand, nor even suspected such action was a possibility, Roland understood he was directly responsible for his death.

After a time, he got up and began walking through the castle looking for Sinan. He found him again in the room of leisure.

Sinan looked up at him and spoke. "You feel you have betrayed him."

"I have abandoned the faith of my birth. I have caused the death of a fellow Christian."

Sinan replied solemnly, "My son, you are no longer a Christian."

He waited for the gravity of that statement to penetrate fully into Roland's consciousness and then continued, "You have chosen the road of Truth. Jesus himself told you to let the dead bury the dead and continue your own journey to the Light."

Sinan paused. Then he looked into his student's troubled eyes and spoke again.

"The time that has been given to you for self-doubt has passed."

Roland was silent.

CHAPTER 32

Roland kept to himself for several days, meditating and thinking over the last two years as a student of this mysterious teacher. He at last understood that Sinan was right. He had no more doubts about his path.

His mind and heart were filled with sorrow about Pierre, but clearly the Templar sergeant had behaved in a way that would have had disastrous and far-reaching consequences. Had he successfully left Al-Kaph and incited Guillaume, Henry would have had little choice but to act. Would he have abandoned his alliance with Sinan and thereby weakened the Crusader position? Would he have attacked Al-Kaph, plunging the region into war?

Would King Henry have arrested Roland and been forced by pressure from Guillaume and others to submit him to interrogation and torture? It was one thing for the king to trust a diplomat and childhood friend; it was quite another for him to countenance a traitor and a heretic.

As far as Roland was concerned, he was neither. He understood that he was, in fact, a sincere seeker after a Greater Truth whose quest had been regularly rewarded by his relationship with, and exposure to, the teachings of Sinan. He knew he was growing under the tutelage of the Assassin king, and anyone who jeopardized or threatened his pursuit of this greater Wisdom was an enemy.

He was also aware that his friendship with his Master was a stabilizing force for the survival of the European mission in the Holy Land—a politically advantageous relationship for his countrymen—exactly as Henry had hoped it might be. Pierre's precipitous behavior was in direct opposition to the wider Crusader interests, no matter how well-intentioned or innocent his motivations may have been.

Roland realized he had come through this ordeal of uncertainty and was at peace with his conscience. While he was certainly not happy about Pierre's death, he accepted it as a necessary event over which he had no control. He emerged from his isolation and joined Sinan.

The two men walked outside to a large field beyond the walls of the castle. Sinan carried a bow. A quiver filled with arrows was slung over his shoulder. They stopped by a brook. Far in the distance was a target, a wooden disk painted red.

Sinan asked, "That target . . . can you hit it?"

"It is beyond the useful range of a longbow. It is an impossible shot."

"Try it."

Sinan handed the bow and an arrow to Roland. Roland took careful aim. He shot, but missed by many yards.

As he turned to face Sinan, Roland could see Aisha standing a considerable distance behind them. She was drawing an arrow. She released it, and they watched as it soared skyward. Roland was incredulous when the arrow slammed into the target.

Sinan explained, "You were correct. You could never have made that shot, Roland. But you can allow the arrow and the target to unite, guided by your will.

"Let us put your meditation training to practical use again. Take an arrow."

Roland pulled an arrow from the quiver and notched it in the bow. He breathed deeply and studied the target far in the distance. He lifted the bow, drew the bowstring, took aim, and followed Sinan's instructions.

"Focus on the target, the bow, the arrow, and your intention. All else will disappear. There is no sun, no sky, no earth, no brook. Your mind is one-pointed."

Roland stood with absolute stillness, hearing only the sound of Sinan's voice. He then relaxed the bowstring and lowered the bow as he listened with deep concentration to Sinan's words.

"When you next draw the bow, your stance will be firm. Your

body is the platform to steady the shot. The forward pressure of the bow in your left hand will be perfectly offset by the pull of your right hand as it holds the arrow against the bowstring. The point of the arrow is aligned with the target. Let the longing of the target adjust the arc of the arrow that they may be united. See only the target."

Roland entered the state of mind he knew from his meditation practices. He exhibited a profound inner stillness as he continued to listen to the instructions.

"You are completely relaxed. You will raise the bow and aim the shot. Then you will test your aim by closing your eyes, breathing evenly, and checking to see that the arrow has remained in perfect alignment with the target when you next open your eyes.

"You may, if necessary, adjust your position to refine your aim rather than trying to correct it by using muscle tension.

"Your sole concern is to let neither mental nor physical interference disrupt either your shooting platform or your natural point of aim. You will release the arrow to its destination. In your mind, it has already found the target."

Roland raised the bow into the firing position again, drew back on the bowstring, and took aim.

He closed his eyes for a moment, breathed deeply, opened his eyes, slightly adjusted his position by moving his feet, rechecked his aiming point, and fired. The arrow slammed into the wooden target within inches of Aisha's arrow.

CHAPTER 33

Roland came into the room of leisure one night and found Sinan and Aisha deep in conversation. He was aware of a palpable air of sadness.

"My son, King Henry has written to me in response to my letter informing him of the death of Pierre Duchien. Your time here has been a gift to all of us, but it draws to a close. You must prepare to return to your regiment. I do not anticipate your being able to return."

Roland was disheartened.

"I will be lost without your guidance, your friendship."

Turning to Aisha, he lost his self-control.

"Your love."

Sinan spoke sadly, yet pensively.

"My son, you will never be separated from us. Our bonds endure through time. You now have the keys to reach the very source of Wisdom itself."

"Will I ever see you again?"

Aisha replied, "Whenever you peer within yourself, you will never be apart from us. Neither time nor distance exists in the realm of the soul."

Sinan amplified her thought.

"As you dedicate your life to the search for divine knowledge and seek to extend the Chain of Light to worthy seekers among your own people, it will only draw us closer.

"You will face trials and tribulation. We shall ever watch over you. You go therefore with my blessing, my love, and my protection.

"And—at the end—though your body may fall by sword or by fire, by age or by illness, you will extract the golden essence of your Self and rise in splendor through the realms beyond Earth. And there we shall greet each other again."

Aisha placed her hand on Roland's shoulder as they looked into each other's eyes.

Later that night Roland was restless and unable to sleep. He rose, walked out of the castle, and made his way alone into the hills. A full moon lit the rocky path.

Roland stopped suddenly. He was certain he heard the voice of Sinan. Puzzled, he walked toward the sound.

By the light of the moon, he saw Sinan speaking in a strange tongue with what appeared to be a green bird glowing with supernatural light. The bird was perched on a tree branch at eye level with Sinan, who appeared to be fully engaged in their mysterious dialogue. Roland observed in silence.

At last, somewhat shaken, he backed away and returned to the castle.

The next morning he and Sinan were eating breakfast. Roland was embarrassed but spoke up.

"Master, last night I came upon a strange sight. I believe I saw you in conversation with a glowing green bird."

Sinan nodded and smiled, "For many years, I have been visited by the spirit of Hasan *ala dhikrhi as salam.* He appears to me in the form of a radiant bird. We discuss the Mysteries and review our mutual responsibilities.

"Last night, you were invited to join us because we were discussing you."

Roland was astonished. As if on cue, Aisha entered the room.

Sinan continued, "I have long concealed a prophecy from you, but will share it now. As I mentioned at your initiation, upon the death of Hasan his disciples made a death mask from which the Golden Head was fashioned.

"However, Hasan foretold the branching of our Order far beyond the confines of Alamut, Al-Kaph, and the Nizari community.

"Thus, a second Golden Head was fashioned. I was entrusted with protecting it until the time came to pass it on to our rightful representative. It is you who will carry the Gnosis to the West."

Roland gazed at Sinan with surprise and humility.

"The conversation you witnessed last night was the final affirmation. We intend to pass on the second Golden Head to the leader of the western branch of our Order. I ask you to share with me the burden that has, until now, been mine alone."

Sinan reached down beside him and picked up a jewel-encrusted box. All three rose. Sinan handed the box to Roland. Roland was speechless with emotion and anticipation. He opened the box and saw the second radiant head. He looked into Sinan's eyes, which reflected the golden color of the sacred icon.

CHAPTER 34

Roland and his Assassin bodyguard, Ahmed, were saddling up in the courtyard. Aisha, eyes moist, walked up to Roland as the fidai quietly stepped away to give them privacy.

Aisha was holding a single rose. She looked up into Roland's eyes.

"All is in readiness?"

"Yes, I'm afraid so."

Aisha looked at the ground as they stood in silence. Then she looked back up at Roland.

"The rose is a symbol of the unfolding of the soul."

She handed the flower to him.

"May its perfume always remind you of your time here . . . and of me."

Roland looked at the rose and then at Aisha. They embraced tenderly. Then Aisha turned and walked away.

Roland looked longingly at the woman in whose presence his heart first opened.

PART SIX

SUSPICION AND SURVEILLANCE

CHAPTER 35

Guillaume looked down from the crest of a hill in the country-side outside Acre. He was leading a Templar patrol of twenty men. In the distance they observed a Saracen encampment. A sergeant in uniform rode up for orders.

Guillaume growled, "These are the Infidels who ambushed the German pilgrims yesterday."

He studied the group below.

"Prepare the men to attack!"

The sergeant was reluctant to disagree with his commander, but felt bound to share his concerns about a reckless charge.

"Sir, they don't look like warriors. More like members of a merchant caravan."

With a zealot's gleam in his eye, Guillaume ignored the comment, drew his sword, and shouted to the men in a maniacal voice, "Death to the enemies of Christ!"

The Templars charged. The Saracens were mercilessly slaughtered. Their lack of skill with weapons clearly confirmed they were not fighting men.

Soon after Guillaume and the patrol returned to the Templar headquarters, Roland arrived at the end of his journey from Al-Kaph. He bade farewell to Ahmed, dismounted, secured his horse, and ascended the stone stairway leading to the heavy wooden door of the commander's office. He was admitted just as a sweaty Guillaume was removing his armor. A large crucifix hung on the wall behind the commander—as foreign an icon of the higher states of consciousness Roland had experienced as he could imagine.

Guillaume spoke curtly, "I'm relieved that your stay at that heathen fortress is finally over. It's time you returned to your own kind and your duties here."

He searched Roland's face and continued.

"The death of Pierre Duchien troubles us all. I am sure it was a great blow to you."

Roland bowed his head.

Then Guillaume paused, deciding to feign friendship and sympathy, but his message was clear.

"I don't question your loyalty or devotion to duty. I would only remind you that we Templars are of one mind and one purpose, and that purpose is to kill the Infidel!"

"I have found, sir, that not all Saracens wish us ill."

"Young man, we are warriors of an angry God whose kingdom and birthplace are defiled by idolaters and heathen! Never forget that. You are dismissed."

CHAPTER 36

Roland had been back in Acre for over a week. He was happy to be reunited with Andre and Landro, while remaining depressed about leaving Sinan and Aisha. He was attempting to make the best of his new situation. He knew he must accept the change in his circumstances as a phenomenon from which he could draw further insight into his true destiny. To do so, however, he needed to open himself again to the present and grow beyond his yearning for Al-Kaph.

As he ruminated on these matters in his quarters, he heard some activity in the courtyard and went outside to witness a disturbing sight. A Templar sergeant on horseback was leading an Assassin on foot. The captive's hands and feet were shackled by chains. Both men were followed by two more guards on horseback. Roland arrived as the prisoner was being taken to the dungeon of the fortress and was only able to see his back. He noted Guillaume hurrying toward the dungeon and Roland followed along with several other Templars.

When they had all assembled in the dank dungeon below the ground level of the fortress, he recognized Tafir, a young fidai he knew from Al-Kaph. Tafir was one of the Assassins constantly moving in and out of his acquaintance during his time with Sinan. While they were never particularly close, Roland had always felt a certain fondness for him, intuiting Tafir to be a brave and resolute warrior. He knew him to be one of Sinan's close circle of trusted disciples. He was alarmed by the peril into which the fidai had fallen and looked at him with sympathy and concern. Tafir saw Roland and sought to reassure him with a glance in return.

Roland and Andre stood along the wall of the chamber. Guillaume took a position in front of the prisoner indicating he would personally conduct the interrogation. The observant commander had caught the glimpse of sympathy between Roland and Tafir and was determined to show no mercy.

The Assassin exhibited a complete lack of fear, remaining silent. As his clothing was ripped off by a guard, his initiate's black cord, identical to the one Roland had received from Sinan, could be seen around his waist.

A branding iron was glowing in the fire and assorted knives and other implements of torture were being set down on a long table by assistants.

Guillaume bellowed with sadistic glee to all present, "Now you will see how we deal with Infidel spies!"

Roland was torn. He struggled between his desire to help the Assassin, his duty to Andre and the fledgling circle of Templar adepts, and the reality of his own survival. His inner conflict was reflected on his face as he wondered what, if anything, he could do.

Tafir soon resolved this dilemma.

Tafir thought back with pride to that monumental day at Al-Kaph when the Master had honored him with a personal summons to his private garden. He knew Sinan was his link to the spiritual center of his aspiration—that Sinan was his direct connection with Allah. Raised since childhood in his care, Tafir had loved and trusted his Master since his earliest memory.

Sinan explained that he was sending Tafir on a dangerous mission to Acre. He needed Tafir to assess Roland's situation. If he could, he should establish direct contact with Roland and question him personally. If that was impossible because of circumstances, Tafir should at least determine if Roland seemed to be moving freely about, or if he appeared to be monitored and under suspicion for the death of Pierre Duchien, or even incarcerated.

Sinan understood that Duchien's death, under his care, had cast a dark shadow over the relationship between the Assassins and King Henry. It was undoubtedly the proximate cause of Roland being recalled. While no open hostility was yet threatened, he knew Roland's treatment on his return to Acre would indicate the immediate future for the Assassin/Crusader peace treaty.

Sinan handed Tafir a small wax ball.

"Your mission will be dangerous. You will need to get close to the Templar fortress. If you are captured by the Crusaders, you will be tortured and killed. Hide this ball inside your mouth. Bite down on it if you find yourself with no recourse. You will thus deprive your enemies of the pleasure of watching you suffer."

Aware of his failure to accomplish the objective, Tafir bit down on the wax ball, releasing poison into his bloodstream. The Templars were all preoccupied with their preparations for the anticipated gruesome hours ahead. They checked and rechecked their various tools and confirmed the sequence of the evening's activities with Guillaume. Everyone seemed to be in motion and focused on best fulfilling his own task.

Unnoticed at first, Tafir's grim face began to register signs of the fast-acting poison. Blood started to flow from his mouth. Soon after, he fell to the ground, convulsed, and died.

Guillaume shouted, "What in the name of God is this?"

A Templar knelt down and opened the prisoner's mouth because of the blood evidence. He inserted gloved fingers and pulled out the remains of the poison capsule. Puzzled at first, he reported to Guillaume.

"Commander, it seems to be a wad of wax or gum mastic."

Suddenly he realized its import.

"It must have held poison ..."

Guillaume spat out in a fury, "Animals!"

Tafir had freed Roland from his predicament. But the damage had been done. Although after years at Al-Kaph it would not be unusual for Roland to recognize the spy, the friendship and alliance implicit in their eye contact was revealing. Guillaume's suspicions of Roland had been further enflamed.

And Roland knew it.

CHAPTER 37

Guillaume was in his office the next day wrestling with the image of Roland and Tafir's sympathetic exchange the night before. Here certainly was treason. How could he probe deeper into this conspiracy? How could he unmask and avert the danger that threatened his command and the lives and souls of the men in his charge?

He thought back to the words of Bernard's letter that had decided the course of his life so long ago. "He does not carry a sword without just cause, for he is a minister of God, and he punishes malicious men . . ." He knew he must relentlessly pursue the answers to the doubts that tormented him.

He summoned two young Templars to meet him. Gaston de Navarre and Philippe de Chartres stood rigidly at attention, nervously waiting for their commander to speak.

"I find no pleasure in crying 'treason,' but something is clearly being concealed here. There is double-dealing and treachery— I am certain of it!"

Philippe, unsure of whether he and Gaston were under suspicion themselves, weakly asked, "Of what do you speak, sir?"

"You are bound by silence on this matter. I have concerns regarding Roland and Andre. They may pose a serious threat to our Order."

There was a look of relief and astonishment on the faces of the two men. Happy to have confirmed they were not being disciplined for an unknown infraction, they were shocked to learn that such illustrious senior knights as Roland and Andre were under scrutiny. Guillaume softened his tone.

"I am concerned for their welfare; they may be misguided. If we can discover their error, we can lead them to recognize it, confess, and repent. They are our brothers. We must help them if they have deviated from the true path of the Christian knight. On the other hand, perhaps I am wrong and there is no problem. After some investigation, we may be able to confirm their innocence and put our minds at ease."

He paused and wondered if these two recruits had the requisite skills and cunning to deceive the suspects. On the other hand, he knew their youth and apparent guilelessness might well mislead Roland and Andre into not suspecting they could be his agents.

"I want you to cultivate friendships with both of them and learn what you can of their views and activities. Do not make your interest too apparent. Is that understood?"

The two spies nodded in agreement, enthusiastically rising to the challenge of receiving a personal mission from their leader.

CHAPTER 38

Elsewhere that day, Roland and Andre were on patrol. They both knew the events of the night before had further aroused Guillaume's suspicions and hostilities. And that his frustration over the thwarted interrogation would make him an even more dangerous adversary.

They stopped to water their horses and talk out of earshot of the sergeants who accompanied them.

Andre observed, "The surveillance will be relentless now. We'll have to be more discreet than ever."

Roland replied, "If fate throws a knife at you, there are two ways of catching it—by the blade or by the hilt. We'll catch Guillaume's knife by its handle and use it in a counterthrust."

"How so?"

"He will certainly employ fellow Templars as informants. They'll try to get us to incriminate ourselves. So we'll use his own spies against him. For now, we'll suspend any outreach to others. Please warn Landro to adopt the greatest caution. When approached by Guillaume's agents, you and I will feign contempt for the Saracens and admiration for our commander. When suspicions have died down, we can resume our efforts."

The surveillance had begun. The next night Andre was in the armory cleaning his weapons. Philippe walked in, removed a gauntlet, and attempted to strike up a conversation.

The innocent youth, barely out of his teens, began, "You have to admire that Saracen spy in a way. He took his own life rather than talk. I guess that's honorable from one point of view."

In his best imitation of Guillaume, Andre thundered back, "Saracens have no honor! The prisoner took his own life simply because he feared torture. No Christian warrior would show that kind of cowardice."

"I only meant . . ."

"It surprises me that you would speak so highly of an Infidel."

"No, you misunderstand, sir! I only . . ."

Andre interrupted Philippe, turning imperiously on his heels. "Excuse me. I have the night watch."

Later that evening, Andre and Roland walked along the battlements of the Templar fortress, looking out over the city of Acre. Andre filled Roland in on his conversation with Philippe.

Laughing, Roland spoke, "His wits are duller than usual! Could he have been more obvious?"

Andre, feeling jubilant, mocked their commander.

"The evil Guillaume—thwarted again!"

Roland became serious. Watching Tafir take his own life, knowing the intentions of the Templars that night, confirming the suspicion under which he and Andre labored—had all been sobering and chilling. He was under no illusion about the danger they were facing or the importance of their mission. Sinan had charged him with a life-and-death task. The life or death could be his own or, worse yet, that of the men for whom he was responsible. Critical thinking was now an enormously important strategic asset for both himself and the others.

"No Andre, not evil. Convictions make men blind. Guillaume is a victim of superstition. He confuses the teachings of Christ with the religion that took Christ's name. We who understand this must be especially clear in our own minds and expression."

Andre contemplated Roland's words as he gazed over the city.

CHAPTER 39

A storm was raging in the night and thunder rumbled in the distance. Roland sat motionless at his desk in meditation, staring by the light of a single candle at a golden disk bearing an occult symbol.

There was a knock at the door. It flew open before he could rise to answer. It was Gaston, the second of Guillaume's rather hapless spies. His rude entrance was obviously calculated to allow him to discover something nefarious going on.

"Oh—sorry! I do apologize for barging in like this."

Roland picked up the candlestick and moved toward the intruder, throwing the incriminating disk into the shadows.

Gaston explained his purpose, handing Roland a folded parchment.

"A message has arrived for you."

Roland took the letter, opened it, and began reading with a look of growing concern.

The next morning he was in Guillaume's office with a pained expression in his eyes.

"My mother has died, and my father is in ill health. He requests that I return to France."

Guillaume's hostility toward Roland was momentarily suspended by the news. Having lost both his own parents in recent years, he allowed a tone of sympathy to color his conversation.

"I am sorry to hear this, Roland. God rest her soul. How much time do you think you need?"

Relieved by the unexpected humanity of Guillaume's response, Roland replied, "Nine months, perhaps, sir."

"This is highly irregular . . ."

Guillaume quickly considered the situation, and especially the potential leverage Roland's absence would give him.

"I will grant you six months' leave out of respect for your

eminent father and his services to the Crown. When will you depart?"

"A pilgrim galley leaves for Venice in three days' time. From Venice, I will travel overland to our home in Avignon."

Guillaume resumed his normal imperious manner.

"Very well then. Six months. Dismissed."

"Thank you, sir."

As Roland exited, Gaston and Philippe emerged from the next room where they had been listening.

Guillaume's voice registered elation.

"Roland's absence will be highly useful to us! Without his leadership, the others will quickly falter and disperse."

Having made travel preparations, Roland readied himself to board a pilgrim galley soon to sail from the Acre harbor. As he was about to take his leave, he bid farewell to an apprehensive Andre.

"For now, we must remain few and secret—out of wisdom, not fear. You and Landro should continue your work together. You can remain sensitive to the spiritual yearnings of any who may be fit to join us. But please use the greatest caution. When I return there will be time enough to reassess our efforts."

PART SEVEN

THE TEACHINGS OF THE CATHARS

CHAPTER 40

King Henry rode in through the massive gate of Acre. Guillaume had been informed of his imminent arrival by Henry's scouts not long before and hurried to prepare his men for the royal visitor. Henry greeted the commander in the courtyard with a look of concern. They immediately removed themselves to the privacy of Guillaume's office.

The death of Pierre Duchien weighed heavily on the king. Was Sinan telling him the truth about it being an accident or had Pierre been murdered? The still unknown motive for the Assassin slaying of Conrad of Montferrat contributed to Henry's anxiety. Had they acted as agents of King Richard as some believed, or was there a more mundane explanation? Conrad had seized a Nizari vessel, confiscated its goods, and killed its crew. Sinan was unlikely to let such behavior stand unpunished.

Henry was understandably on edge. Did a dark cloud of betrayal hang over a treaty that had already resulted in several years of peace? If so, was a regional war on the horizon? He expressed his concerns to Guillaume.

"I need to speak with Roland. Pierre Duchien's death forces me to reassess my alliance with Sinan. I need first-hand information."

Guillaume was surprised to learn that Henry was yet unaware of the death of Roland's mother. He knew of the king's closeness with the family and realized the messenger carrying word from Europe to Jerusalem could have been delayed for any number of reasons.

"My liege, Roland left for France just two days ago. His mother died, and his father has taken ill. I extended him a six-month leave to care for his father."

Henry was shaken by this unwelcome and unexpected news.

"I am so sorry to hear this. Count Bertram and the Lady Marie were both very close to me. I appreciate your extending such kindness to their family."

Henry knew that Andre was Roland's closest friend. Andre had sometimes joined him and Roland in play as children. He hoped that Andre might be able to provide some insights based on conversations with Roland.

"Please have Andre brought here. It is possible Roland shared some of his more intimate thoughts with him."

Guillaume was obviously uncomfortable with Andre because of his suspicions about the two knights. But without proof, he knew he had best not mention a word of these concerns to Henry. Reluctantly, he arranged for Andre to be summoned to join them.

Henry greeted Andre easily. Andre was happy to see the king—well aware of the difference between Henry as his former elder playmate and Henry's current status as his liege lord. He sensed immediately that the king was here without malice, that Guillaume had not dared accuse either him or Roland yet. On the other hand, he was acutely aware of Guillaume's suspicions and hostility, and was discomfited by being in such close proximity to him in the small office.

Henry probed Andre for any intelligence he may have gathered from Roland on the cause of Pierre's death. The explanation of "unfortunate accident" that he had received by dispatch from Sinan was, at best, incomplete. Had Roland shared more details? Was it an accident, an illness, or was foul play involved?

Andre was, of course, well aware of the real story, which Roland had confided in him. While Roland knew that Pierre's attempted betrayal was the cause of his death, he remained troubled by the entire experience.

"Roland explained to me that he and Pierre were hunting lions one day in the Nusayri Mountains. An Assassin child had just been killed by a lion outside the castle. Though hunting is forbidden by our Rule, lions are an exception because Saint Peter identified them as a form of the Devil. Roland and Pierre spotted a lion in the distance and were galloping after it when Pierre's horse hit a cleft in the rock and he was thrown. When Roland reached him, he found Pierre's neck had been broken by the fall. The horse's leg was also broken. It was a tragedy that continues to plague Roland's heart."

Henry seemed satisfied by this confirmation of the Assassin king's statement about it being an accident. Guillaume was aware that it agreed with the story Roland had told him and gave a slight nod.

Henry then decided to probe deeper into this current dilemma and asked, "Andre, I am curious to know your opinion. What do you think should be our best course of action with Sinan?"

Guillaume had earlier suggested that Henry violate the truce and attack the Assassins. Had they not murdered Conrad of Montferrat? Was that not sufficient justification for war even though it had occurred five years earlier? Was not Pierre's death, however it may have happened, the most recent example of the spilling of Christian blood? And finally, what was the purpose of the Crusader presence in the Holy Land if not the death of the Infidel?

Andre answered Henry with care. "My liege, Roland and I have had deep discussions about this alliance. We both agree that our continuing treaty with the Assassins is an intelligent approach to the reality of this most dangerous region. We have been able to spend almost three years fortifying ourselves and our position against our numerous enemies without interference from the Assassins. Nor has there been need for us to even devote much thought to them.

"We understand that it was probably necessary for you to recall Roland after Pierre's death. But if we should mount an attack against Al-Kaph and the other Assassin fortresses, it would mean all our resources would be consumed by that effort. That does not seem to either of us to be the wisest course."

Henry respected the younger knight's careful and reasoned insight. He perceived an aptitude for strategic thinking, an ability to move outside of the prejudices and passions that consumed

Guillaume. This was an aspect of Andre of which the king had been previously unaware. He made careful note for the future. He thanked Andre, who then left the room.

Henry spoke first. "For now, I have made my decision. There will be no breaking of my treaty with Sinan."

Guillaume was certainly not pleased, but realized the burden was now his alone. If he could prove his suspicions against Roland and Andre—with irrefutable evidence—Henry would have no choice but to act. While the king may have a fondness for both these traitors, unassailable proof would demonstrate his folly in trusting men who had essentially become agents of Sinan. Guillaume was determined to get to the bottom of this matter once and for all.

CHAPTER 41

Roland was focused on a series of conflicting thoughts and emotions as the ship sailed on. He kept to himself, remaining apart from the other travelers.

Childhood memories of his mother and father filled his consciousness, as did his present concern for his father. His home had been filled with love; he had cared deeply for both his parents.

On the other hand, he was grateful for the time and solitude the five weeks at sea would afford him to carefully review the evolving and increasingly complex situation in Acre. Images of Sinan and Aisha remained at the forefront of his musings as well, and he devoted much thought and emotional energy to them as he sailed.

Eventually, without incident, the ship docked at Venice. Roland made his way to a stable where he purchased a horse to begin the long overland journey to Avignon. The nearly three-week trip took him through gentle countryside, thick forest, and the foothills of the Alps. He continued on through southern France toward Avignon.

Riding through a light rain along a country road just outside Avignon, he encountered a traveling covered carriage. It was stuck in the muddy road with a wheel lodged in a deep rut. An elderly driver and two women looked on helplessly.

The younger of the women, about twenty-five, spoke first.

"Might we request your assistance, sir?"

Roland was enchanted. Her dark red hair, white skin, brown eyes, and gentle but noble bearing captivated him.

He replied, "At your service, my ladies."

The elder woman responded, "Thank you, young man."

She seemed a person of strength and character. Her gentle tone exuded a humility that Roland found appealing. She was about fifty, a little younger than his mother, but her kindness and overall mien touched a familiar chord in his heart.

The single work horse was not strong enough to pull the wheel out of the mud. Roland harnessed his own horse to the carriage to help with the task. Together, the two horses—with the joint efforts of Roland and the driver pushing from behind— were able to free the wheel. It was a dirty job. Roland's clothes were filthy, but he was happy to have been of help.

Much relieved by their success, the younger woman thanked him and introduced herself and her companion.

"My name is Arianne. This is my aunt, Iolande. We have traveled from our home in Albi to visit relatives here in Avignon. We are in your debt, sir!"

"I am Roland, on leave from service in the Holy Land because of my mother's recent death and my father's ill health."

Arianne expressed her sympathy for his loss and then noticed the signet ring on his finger. She was surprised.

"Your father is Bertram, Comte de Provence! Sir, I apologize for pressing you into such coarse and unbecoming work!"

Roland laughed, and looked down at his muddy clothing.

"I suppose I hardly look the part of a nobleman!"

Arianne smiled and her eyes lit up.

"As it is said, 'A horse of good breed is not dishonored by his saddle.'"

Roland was captivated by this well-spoken and self-assured young woman. She was, in turn, attracted to the handsome knight. Roland's rigidity, his previous discomfort with women, and lack of sophistication had long since been dissolved in the alembic of Aisha. He was a very different person than one might expect to meet along a country road in southern France or, for that matter, anywhere else in medieval Europe.

Politely, he turned to Iolande.

"May I inquire where you will be staying while in our city?"

"On the Rue des Études—the house next to the Latin school."

"If my father's health permits, may I invite you both to dine at our estate? If his condition prevents it, I will send word."

Arianne was delighted, "We would be honored, my lord."

CHAPTER 42

Avignon was an attractive and bustling city of some 5,000 residents. Its St. Benezet Bridge, opened thirty years earlier, spanned the Rhone. The Cathedrale Notre-Dame-des-Doms and its other well-designed architectural works highlighted the simple elegance of its setting. On the trade route between Italy and Spain, Avignon enjoyed an active commercial prosperity.

The modest house in which Arianne, her father Simon, and Iolande were staying while in town was owned by relatives who were Cathar co-religionists. They had left Avignon for a preaching mission in the Carcassonne area and were happy to know their home was being cared for in their absence—which might extend to several months if all went well.

The Cathars of the Languedoc were an intensely spiritual group, living in simplicity. Their clergy, the Perfect or *Parfait*, were a non-professional class whose humble lifestyles were sustained by their own efforts and the charity of the community. Adept in the healing arts, pious in their behavior, undemanding, and generous, they were an accepted part of the extended community of the Languedoc.

In the common room of the Avignon home, Arianne and Iolande were conversing with a group of Cathar women who were happy to welcome them to town. They chatted as they worked together at their needlepoint designs by the remaining light of the late afternoon sun.

Iolande was delighted to be welcoming the polite young knight to dinner later that evening. Some days earlier, Roland had made contact with them. His message said that while he was relieved to have returned to his father's side, because of Bertram's weakened condition it would be better for Roland to join them in town first. Later, when his father was fully recovered, they could come to visit his family's countryside estate.

Iolande had been impressed by Roland's character during their encounter on the muddy road. "He was not arrogant like so many young knights. There was a gentleness about him."

Arianne was looking forward to Simon's arrival.

"I know Father will enjoy meeting him. I sense they will have many things to discuss and appreciate together . . ."

She was interrupted by a firm knock at the door. It was a messenger with an envelope. Arianne opened the letter and shared its contents with the women.

"Sir Roland sends word that Count Bertram is near death."

Arianne wrestled with her thoughts for a moment, then made her decision. She addressed the messenger.

"Please take me to your master."

CHAPTER 43

When Arianne arrived at the manor, the messenger led her to Roland who was sitting in a chair beside his father's bed. Count Bertram was delirious. He was in his late sixties and appeared to be on the very doorsteps of death.

Roland rose to greet Arianne. He walked over to her and whispered, "The doctors have given up all hope."

Arianne remained firm in the decision she had made earlier to take the risk of revealing herself for the good of this young man and his noble father.

"Your father is a man of honor and generosity, much loved by all who know him. I have some knowledge of healing. May I do what I can?"

"Please hurry."

"Ask everyone to leave the room."

Roland complied. Everyone left while he stayed behind.

Arianne had expected him to go as well and was nonplussed by his remaining. She gently spoke, "Please, my lord, if you don't mind."

Roland sensed her reluctance to have him present.

She tried to explain her discomfort.

"My methods are . . . unconventional."

She went on, sheepishly, her voice almost in a whisper.

"Some might consider it witchcraft."

Roland stifled a laugh, "You have nothing to fear from me."

Arianne interpreted his good humor as mockery and responded with anger.

"Do you then think me a gullible provincial, steeped in superstition?"

Roland quickly realized her misinterpretation and tried to assure this brave and generous young woman of his sympathy with her spiritual singularity.

"I am so sorry, my lady. I laughed because I—of all people— am the last person a witch should fear."

Arianne was puzzled. Roland smiled, and she realized from his look that he was hiding some form of knowledge. She accepted the fact that this unusual man continued to intrigue her and asked no further questions. Roland closed the door.

"I am a Cathar—a sect, as you know, that is considered heretical by many. We practice healing arts. I will try to help balance and replenish your father's natural energy."

Arianne first performed a cleansing ritual of the bedroom. She took a silver dagger from its sheath in her bag and stood in the center of the room, entering a state of stillness and deep concentration. She extended her arm and the dagger above her head pointing upward, lowered and aimed it straight in front her to the east. She traced a circle around to the south, the west, the north, and completed it back in the east. She then lowered the dagger and pointed downward. She crossed her arms upon her chest, closed her eyes, and bowed her head.

Roland perceived an aura of lightness within the room, as if the pain and suffering that had been endured there was eased, healed, and purified. Arianne opened her eyes.

She then began the healing ceremony proper. Using a series of hand positions and movements, while intoning a mantra, Arianne's body began to vibrate with energy. Roland felt a surging power coming from her. He recognized it immediately as akin to that holy power with which he himself had become so familiar these past years.

He watched his father break out into a profuse sweat as his body temperature rose to kill off and flush out the infection. At the completion of Arianne's ceremony, the count was sleeping peacefully.

She turned from her patient and looked up at Roland. He met her gaze and felt her strength. She sensed his heightened respect for her power.

"Some men are afraid of a woman's strength."

"Some men."

Roland searched her eyes in the flickering candlelight.

CHAPTER 44

Within a week of Count Bertram's extraordinary recovery, Simon and his sister, Iolande, were in conversation in the Avignon house. Arianne's father was in his mid-fifties with gray hair and beard. He was of medium height, and his handsome features offered genetic witness to the paternity of his beautiful daughter. Arianne burst into the room.

"He's here!"

She opened the door to Roland. Simon rose in greeting.

"Thank you for coming, my son! Does your father rest well?"

"He does, thanks to your daughter."

"And God's grace! We have prepared a simple meal. Please join us."

Cheeses, fruits, and vegetables were laid out on the table with an aesthetic simplicity. Per Cathar belief, no meat was present.

"My daughter tells me you've spent considerable time in the Holy Land—and that you hold sympathy for our, shall we say, 'unorthodox' teachings."

Roland's eyes lit up.

"I am no stranger to 'unorthodox.'"

He continued, "I served as an ambassador at the fortress of a Saracen adept named Sinan. He instructed me in techniques for stilling the mind and body while peering inward to see the Light of God. We worked with spiritual energies very similar to those Arianne used with my father."

Simon replied, "I am delighted to hear this! We Cathars also seek the sacred truth of the soul within. We believe that a veil separates us from the Inner Light of God, and that by certain practices, we may learn of God's direction for us."

Arianne interjected, "I am curious . . . How did this Saracen adept regard Jesus?"

"To begin with, Sinan is no typical Muslim. He rejects much of the structure of the Islamic faith. But his view of Jesus is similar indeed to that of other educated Saracens. Jesus is one of their prophets, like Abraham, Moses, and Muhammad. But they don't believe that Jesus was God, or the son of God, or that he died for our sins upon the cross."

Simon was surprised and amused.

"You have much to learn of our doctrine! For while we believe Jesus to have been divine, we do not believe he died on a cross either. Nor do we venerate the crucifix."

Iolande joined the conversation.

"We believe Jesus to have been a purely spiritual being— an emissary of the Light, not unlike an angel. He was sent by God in His mercy to guide us to perfection by teaching spiritual practices that lead to personal salvation and liberation."

Roland began to sense the enormous impact his chance meeting with Arianne and Iolande was going to have on his understanding of Truth.

"I have many questions for you . . ."

Simon was pleased.

"My daughter was right. You are, indeed, a serious man. Let's walk together after we finish our meal."

Simon had taken an immediate liking to Roland. While he was no stranger to the power of a first impression, this was unexpected. He felt as if there were a long-cultivated and easy familiarity between himself and this bright young man.

After their dinner, Simon and Roland strode along a picturesque tree-lined street that ran beside the Rhone River. It was late in the day. The sun seemed to be leisurely surveying his daytime kingdom before beginning the evening's journey through the realms of night.

Simon began a more detailed explanation of Cathar history and doctrine. Roland was surprised to learn that Catharism traced its roots to Persia, the birthplace of the Assassins.

The third-century Dualist heresy of Mani was its main source. Mani had been martyred for his beliefs by the religious authorities of his day. He built his teachings on the doctrines of

Zoroaster, who had preached as long ago as a millennium before him.

Simon mentioned that the famed Christian theologian Saint Augustine had been a member of a Manichaean sect in Egypt for nine years during the fourth century and wrote critically of them after converting to Christianity. However, it was the tenth-century Bulgarian Bogomils who were the most immediate predecessors of the French Cathars. They had spread their Dualist teachings first to Germany and then to the Languedoc.

Unfamiliar with the term, Roland asked Simon, "What is the meaning of 'Dualism'?"

"We believe there is a spiritual war between God and the Devil for the soul of humankind. It is the war between Good and Evil.

"Some Dualists believe that God and Satan are exactly equal in strength and that their battle extends through all time. We Cathars reject this idea. We believe God is the stronger of the two and will eventually defeat the Devil and his kingdom. We believe this will come about as more people learn to extend our spiritual powers in line with our divine destiny."

"We are hated by the Church. Sadly, the spiritual founder of your own Order was opposed to us. Bernard of Clairvaux visited here some sixty years ago and preached ceaselessly against us. He felt we should be excommunicated."

Roland was disappointed to hear this, but he was well aware of the superstition and ignorance that ran through both the Church and his Templar Order.

Simon continued, "The Church regards us as competition."

He smiled at Roland as he added, "While we are more than happy to tolerate them and their beliefs, they refuse to follow our open-minded example."

Roland laughed as he imagined Guillaume joining their conversation.

Roland felt a kinship with the ideas he was hearing. What had been lacking in his experience with Sinan was the cultural bond he shared with Simon. There was a familiarity to Simon's beliefs that fit in with the themes of his upbringing. Their mutual backgrounds as Christians allowed for a commonality that Roland had not found in the exotic realm of the Assassin Master.

Simon next discussed a central tenet of the Cathar faith that was immediately of the deepest significance to Roland.

"We Cathars reject the doctrine of vicarious atonement. The idea of the blood of an innocent person atoning for our sins is repugnant to our principles of justice and fairness. We cleanse ourselves of sin by the work of internal purification."

Roland spoke from his core. "The sacrifice of Jesus for my sins has always troubled me. It is perverse to allow another to pay for what I have done."

Simon's teaching was helping to fill in certain gaps in Roland's understanding of his personal quest. Roland had deliberately set aside such questions while at Al-Kaph. It was, in fact, easy to do so at the time because of the rapidity of his learning process with Sinan and the universality of what they had been exploring together.

It now seemed to him that here with Simon and the Cathars, he would find answers to some unresolved issues.

But he was puzzled as he tried to grasp how Simon could square his rejection of vicarious atonement with his devoted embrace of Christianity.

"Please help me to understand something. The self-sacrifice of Jesus for humanity is the Church's central teaching."

Roland was about to be even more surprised.

"We Cathars regard the Roman Church as a false church that has turned from the true path of God. It has twisted Jesus's teachings to serve its own ambitions. We believe it enchains souls to this world of sin."

Simon was aware of the stunning nature of this revelation to an outsider, even one as sophisticated as Roland appeared to be.

Roland pondered the statement for some moments. He

stopped and looked at Simon. The Church was the bellwether of the medieval world. Despite his own expanded awareness, Simon's words were so alien to his life conditioning he was momentarily taken aback.

"Sir, I have never heard of anyone so openly rejecting the authority of the Church. This is something I must take the time to examine."

Simon signaled his appreciation for Roland's thoughtfulness and continued with his exposition of Cathar doctrine.

"We believe the deception is far more pervasive than even that, my son. The evil prince of this planet has created manifold temptations to lure us from the truth. The Dark Power rules this world and everything in it. All matter is debased and corrupt. We Cathars regard life as a prison and all that binds us to it as evil. Our only hope is to be found in the ascetic practices designed to break and transcend the bonds of existence."

Simon gestured toward the scenic beauty of the river.

"This beauty is our prison. Our very bodies are the prison of our souls. Love, friendship, and joy are all chains that bind us to this evil world. This is why we reject marriage and child-bearing. Who dares continue this evil charade of manifestation by imposing physical life on another divine soul? It is all the Devil's realm. We refuse to compromise ourselves."

Roland stopped short.

"Forgive me, sir, but this is a very dark viewpoint."

He perceived at once that the Cathar belief was itself subject to error. Whatever he learned from his new friends would need to be tested against the standard of a Truth that challenged all orthodoxies, including this one.

Roland also came to an important new understanding. There was a spiritual hierarchy of which he had been previously unaware. Sinan held the most elevated rank in that progression. While Roland may have felt certain cultural gaps in their interaction, he had never discerned an error in his Master's teaching.

Simon was clearly not the spiritual equal of Sinan. Roland had much to share in return that would be of equal value to his new friend. They would learn from each other.

Roland spoke up with all the passion of his own quest for Truth.

"As we look out upon this beautiful scene, do you truly believe it to be evil? Do you suspect that the sun whose warmth caresses our skins is a herald of the Devil? Is this flower an agent of sin? Is your love for your daughter a chain? And—if I might be so bold—was your love for her mother a wicked thing?"

Simon plunged deeply into the memories of his beloved Jeanne. How happy they had been together. How much joy they had shared. The miracle of Arianne's birth and the love within their family had brought an ecstatic joy to Simon that could only be compared in its intensity with the love he felt for God.

He had asked himself many questions at that time and struggled to understand the doctrinal compatibility of his own powerful feelings. Was it possible, he wondered, that after Jeanne's death he had allowed himself to make an almost intellectually dishonest peace with the Cathar idea that her very presence and the joy they shared were examples of the insubstantiality of the physical world?

"I do love my daughter, as I loved her mother, and perhaps in this I err and wander from the teachings of my own faith. For it is our belief that everything in this created world is an impure illusion designed to enslave the spirit to the flesh."

"I cannot accept that, sir. Nor do I believe that you truly do. I see too much love in your eyes. I believe that love is a sacrament, a gift of God. It is neither evil nor a delusion. Indeed, it is one of humankind's greatest blessings."

The two men looked at each other, then continued their walk in silence.

CHAPTER 45

As the sun shone through a dazzling cloudless sky, Roland entered the city park where he had arranged to meet Arianne. He saw her waiting near a low stone wall and his heart rejoiced at the sight of her.

"Shall we walk together?"

She took his arm as they strode along the flower-lined pathways through the beautifully cultivated and manicured greenery of the park.

"The time I've spent with you and your father has been wonderful."

Arianne replied, "I agree. And my father so enjoys your company."

"Arianne, some of your beliefs ring true to me—rejection of vicarious atonement and the cross, certainly. But condemning the material world and everything in it as evil is impossible for me to accept! Surely you cannot believe that love is a sin?"

Arianne looked at him with a troubled gaze.

Roland spoke with heartfelt intensity.

"Arianne, love is a sacred force. We should delight in its holiness rather than reject it. Is it wrong for me to appreciate beauty?"

She answered, "I have long wondered whether in rejecting the physical world and Nature, we Cathars have failed to glorify God. Is it for us to say 'no' to God's bounty?"

"I know only this, Arianne. Love is not a sin."

Roland took her hand. Her hair caught the afternoon breeze. A smile came to her lips—an intimate smile, luminous and radiant. She glowed with warmth and with life.

Roland felt the heat of her nearness. She flowed toward him. They surrendered to that sacred force that had drawn them together since their first meeting in the drizzling rain that now felt like aeons ago. His hand swept to the back of her neck as he pressed his lips to hers. A gentle moan escaped her throat.

They were in love and the days that followed were like a multi-colored continuum of the discovery of each other's totality. They enjoyed Avignon—walking, talking, riding, dining, embracing, and laughing. Roland experienced an entirely new sense of inti-macy with which he was totally unfamiliar. He and Arianne seemed to share a one-on-one bonding, an all-encompassing compatibility that extended to all planes: emotional, intellectual, physical, and spiritual. There was no sense of division, separa-tion, or distance. They were as one being composed of two parts, whose individualities could merge into a greater whole together and then separate back into their own discrete selves—as if in the motions of a sacred choreography.

One day Roland entered the Avignon house and found Simon, standing with his back to the room, gazing out a window.

"Sir, I believe you know why I'm here."

Simon turned around.

"I know."

"I love your daughter. The feeling in my heart toward Arianne is the closest I have ever felt to the love I feel for God. This cannot be a sin."

The point hit home with the older man. A tear rolled down his cheek.

"I have seen her happiness in your company. Since the death of her mother, Arianne has rarely smiled. When she's with you, the glow of love rekindles her spirit."

"Father, I ask you for her hand in marriage. Arianne and I both understand why others will consider our love to be both a sin and a doctrinal error. But we must act on our own understanding and accept the demands of God's plan as it reveals itself to our most honest inquiry."

Simon knew this day was coming and had prayed for guidance. He looked fondly at Roland and nodded his head.

"What God has joined together, let not man put asunder."

The two men embraced.

In the secluded garden behind the house, a small group of very happy people gathered with each other one evening. Roland and Arianne stood together as Simon officiated their marriage ceremony. It was a private affair because this union was both a heresy in the eyes of the Cathar community and a mortal violation of the Templar Rule. Yet those present, including Iolande and Count Bertram, were united in a loving spirit of warmth and joy and silent prayers for the health and happiness of the betrothed.

CHAPTER 46

Some weeks had passed since the wedding and an atmosphere of love suffused the small Avignon home. Simon and Iolande shared in the happiness of the newlyweds.

But one evening after dinner Roland sat by the hearth staring past the fire into his own thoughts. Arianne walked over, kissed him, and sat down beside him.

An air of gravity and concentration was evident in his demeanor.

"My darling, we have a decision to make. My period of leave draws to a close. If I fail to return to Acre, I'll be branded a deserter and become a fugitive. I'm prepared for that . . ."

". . . as am I."

He continued, ". . . but it would leave my duty to both Sinan and Andre unfulfilled. Arianne, I feel I must go back, at least for a few months, until Andre is ready to lead in my absence. I have also learned so much from you and your father and your aunt. I need to share this new knowledge with Andre and those who will join us."

He took his beloved into his arms and confessed the contradiction with which he had been wrestling.

"But I have a responsibility to you."

The wise young woman had an absolutely clear understanding of the path ahead and counseled her troubled husband.

"Of course you must go back! There is nothing to discuss. After you've prepared Andre, then you'll return here . . ."

She laughed. ". . . and we'll become fugitives together."

Roland was filled with gratitude for her presence in his life. They kissed.

"My commander Guillaume de Gonneville has long nurtured both suspicion and resentment toward me because of the two years I spent with Sinan. He is perceptive enough to sense that

I was, in fact, changed by my experience at Al-Kaph. It will be better for everyone if I leave Acre as soon as possible. It will be easier for Andre and the others to work without my constantly drawing Guillaume's scrutiny."

Early next morning the family gathered together in the front yard. Roland, in uniform, took his leave. Arianne fought back tears as he mounted his horse and rode off.

He traveled the fifty miles from Avignon to the port city of Marseilles and continued by ship to Acre. Roland was again alone. He was able to ponder the most recent chain of events that had delivered him to this new crossroads. Servant of a larger destiny, he went forth once again to answer the summons of a Power before which he stood in awe.

PART EIGHT

INITIATION AND ARREST

CHAPTER 47

The Papal throne room was filled with a splendor of gold, ivory, and marble. Drapes of sensuous velvet, intricate and colorful carpets, statues, and paintings added to the sense of beauty and wealth exuded by this magnificent Roman palace. A massive crucifix with the Corpus Christi stood above the golden throne, decorated with precious stones. The throne itself was set upon a dais approached by marble steps.

Upon that royal seat was a very disturbed Pope Innocent III. Forty-eight years old, he had held the papacy for ten years. His had not been an easy reign. An ambitious pope, he had sought to impose the Vatican hegemony on feudal Europe, envisioning all Christian kings submitting to his leadership. As such, he was an enthusiastic supporter of the Knights Templar, lavishing them with praise and privileges, but ruling them with an iron hand. He understood the Templars as the pope's private army and welcomed the ability to enforce his will with military power. While he still smarted from some of the failures and humiliations his papacy had endured, the depths of the problem to which he was being exposed by his current visitor exceeded the burdens he had already experienced.

A Templar knight, Augustus Montaigno, forty years of age, was kneeling in front of the steps.

Pope Innocent exclaimed in disbelief and irritation. "What then? We have already seen our crusading armies besieging fellow Christians in Zara and attacking our heretic brothers of the Eastern Church in Constantinople. You now suggest I send armies to France to battle heresy among the Cathars?"

Jerusalem had been conquered by the Muslims in 638. It had remained in their hands for some 460 years, until it was successfully liberated during the First Crusade. In the century since, Europe had learned of the great difficulty of holding territory in a distant battle zone. The expense associated with what seemed an endless war had created a great sense of fatigue and dissension among many thoughtful people. Yet, the religious importance of redeeming the Holy Land seemed absolutely clear to Pope Innocent.

But the Fourth Crusade, under his leadership, had been a disaster. The treachery of Venetian merchants had caused his armies to be completely routed from their mission. Instead, they were persuaded to launch attacks against false targets, in fact against Christians. The thought of compounding that insanity with a campaign against southern France was appalling to the pope. He nearly shouted at Augustus.

"Have you perhaps forgotten that the armies of my papacy have yet to do battle with the Saracens?"

Augustus raised his head tentatively and looked upward at the pope.

"Holy Father, until now the Cathar treason has been tolerated in southern France. Yet by God's grace, our brothers in the Paris Temple report a growing zeal among the northern nobility aimed at the heretics of the Languedoc and their supporters."

Innocent commented cynically, "I wonder if such holy zeal may not be tempered with greed."

The wealth of the southern French nobility was legendary. While a very small percentage of the residents of the Languedoc were Cathars, their purity, simplicity, and gentleness had won the hearts of most of their neighbors. People supported them and tolerated their supposedly heretical beliefs with equanimity.

The pope rose and began pacing the dais.

"I am also alarmed by the concerns you bring of problems among the Templars in Acre."

"Your Holiness, the Commander of Antioch has reported a conversation with the Regional Master of Acre, Guillaume de Gonneville. Guillaume fears doctrinal irregularity in a former Templar diplomat to the Saracens. He is investigating the matter and will keep us apprised. We decided you should be aware of the situation because it concerns Roland, the son of your friend Count Bertram of Provence. Roland spent several years on a mission at the court of the Assassin king."

"I have known Roland since he was a child. He has always displayed a bright and inquisitive mind.

"I am not surprised that an ambassador might be soiled by the mud of these Infidels. That we must even converse with them sickens me. Yet I am aware of reality and the need for diplomacy.

"You will keep me informed of any developments regarding Roland and any effect he may have on others."

"And the Cathars, Holy Father?"

"I will consider this matter."

That night, Innocent prayed in his private chapel. As he knelt, he experienced a vision of the Crucifixion. As the sound and image of a nail pounded into Christ's hand resonated within his psyche, the Pope's body jerked painfully.

"Dear God! Have you not suffered enough? Is it possible that we allow your enemies to torment you still? That even your own warriors may be betraying you? That I, your vicar, should be counseled to murder the strays and wanderers in my care? Help me to protect you, O Lord! Help me to serve you. Grant me the wisdom to lead your flock."

Tears streamed down his face.

CHAPTER 48

After Roland's ship docked in the Acre harbor, he made his way south through the city. He came to the promontory jutting out into the Mediterranean on which stood the Templar fortress. He saw Andre in the courtyard as soon as he came through the gate of the castle.

Andre greeted him with an infectious enthusiasm that carried him straight out of the solitude and preoccupation of the long sea journey. Servants carried his belongings to his cell as he and Andre walked together in conversation before heading inside.

"Roland! How long I have awaited your return!"

He leaned over and whispered, "I've brought in three more men!"

"That is excellent, Andre!"

Roland confirmed the safety of the Golden Head that he had left in Andre's care during his travels in France.

In time they entered the castle and walked on to Roland's room.

Andre stood by the door, glancing into the hallway to ensure their privacy. Roland began unpacking.

Roland reported, "I've learned much from my contact with the Cathars. We at last have the missing straw and mortar to build our more complete teaching."

"What have you learned?"

"The Cathars hold an extreme view of the evil of this world and of the body—which I reject. But they are appalled by the splendor and wealth of the Church. They deny that the Church is the true voice of Christ."

"This is blasphemy, my Brother."

"Indeed, but there is more. They reject the idea that Jesus died for our sins upon the cross. They reject the cross as a false symbol."

Andre recoiled.

"But we wear the cross, Roland—on our mantles, around our necks!"

Andre picked up Roland's white Templar mantle and displayed its red cross.

Roland waved his hand dismissively.

"The cross is an ancient symbol. Long before Jesus, it was a sign of Light—the sacred fire that dispels the darkness."

He continued, his voice registering his disgust.

"What the Cathars despise is the crucifix—the cross with Jesus's dead body on it. They consider it a false symbol."

"As you know, the notion of Jesus dying for my sins has long troubled me."

"And me. Even as children, the idea that we could get away with something by letting Jesus suffer in our place was offensive to us both. I am more convinced than ever that only a coward would hide behind an innocent scapegoat."

Roland's voice was filled with passion even as he worked to keep his volume low for their mutual security.

"Our priests counsel us to be weaklings, begging God for forgiveness. Sinan taught me to take pride in myself. God wants companions, Andre, not beggars!"

"Roland, you realize that with these new ideas we are entering an even more unexplored territory. Until now we have sought in our spiritual practices to come closer to God. Now we are taking the liberty of redefining Him."

Roland grasped Andre's shoulder, grateful for his friend's understanding, courage, and companionship on this journey.

Andre shook off his concerns as he gleefully reported on a new success.

"Roland, I have a surprise for you!"

Roland laughed, "A surprise! Andre, you're not one for surprises."

"Judge for yourself!"

Andre looked outside the door again to be sure no one was eavesdropping.

"Tomorrow, after Vespers, ride two miles north of the city. On your right you'll see some Roman ruins—three pillars, the middle pillar higher than the other two. A path leads eastward from there toward the hills. On that path you'll come to a small house. Call out, saying, 'I demand your hospitality!' You will be asked on what road you travel. Answer, 'To Tiphareth.'"

Roland was puzzled, but nodded in agreement. He moved closer to Andre and lowered his voice again.

"Before you go, I too have a surprise." He paused, "In Avignon, I met a woman . . ."

CHAPTER 49

Roland was able to leave the fortress and ride north from Acre at dusk. He came upon the three pillars Andre had mentioned and took the path toward the hills. He approached a small house.

As instructed, he shouted, "I demand your hospitality!"

The door opened and an elderly Jewish man appeared. He looked to be in his seventies and wore the customary long hair and beard of the sect, with a yarmulke on his head and a fringed garment visible at his waist. He queried Roland.

"On what road do you travel?"

"To Tiphareth."

His host smiled and motioned to Roland to dismount.

"Yehuda ben Isaac, at your service. Follow me, my friend."

Roland, leading his horse, followed Yehuda through trees and brush, then into a ravine.

"Tie your horse here. And please put on this blindfold."

Yehuda turned the blindfolded Templar around numerous times to disorient him, then led him up to a rocky outcropping on the side of the hill. He pushed aside some foliage and guided Roland between two boulders.

They entered a large cavern illuminated by torches.

Roland heard Andre's voice calling out.

"You can remove your blindfold now."

Roland took off the blindfold and looked around. He was dumbfounded.

"What is this place?"

"It's our secret temple, our study room, our storehouse, our refuge."

Andre beamed with pride as Roland surveyed the large cavern in disbelief.

"And this is Yehuda, our benefactor—a man well-versed in the Kabbalah, the secret doctrines of the Jews—the knowledge of numbers, words, letters, and names."

Yehuda was enthusiastic.

"Young Andre once rendered me a service that ensured the continued attachment of my head to my body! I am forever in his debt—a fact of which he recently reminded me. This cavern is a token of my appreciation."

Roland looked around more carefully.

"This is not a natural cavern."

"This cavern—and those linked to it by underground passageways—were hewn out by my people hundreds of years ago as a hiding place from the Romans during the rebellion of Simeon Bar-Kochba. Now it's yours, for as long as you have need of it. From what Andre tells me, we walk a similar path. Perhaps we can learn from each other."

Roland asked, "What is Tiphareth?"

"In the secret traditions of my people, Tiphareth is an emanation of power on the Tree of Life. It's an aspect of God. It is the domain of Beauty, and represents the Sun. It bestows light, life, and spiritual rebirth."

"I've heard about aspects of God before. I can see we'll have much to discuss."

Yehuda glanced at Andre, who smiled indulgently.

"Well . . . I'll leave you now."

Yehuda departed the cavern with a bow and the two Templars were alone.

"This is incredible, Andre! You have solved our problem. Now we have a place to work. Well done!"

Roland continued and his voice reflected the solemnity of his thought process.

"But we are walking a dangerous road."

"Do you hesitate, Roland? For myself, I have come to trust the Power we have come to know."

"As have I. But if we are mistaken, we are about to enter the flames of Eternal Damnation—and bring others with us."

"Then God help us to know His Truth."

Roland replied slowly and thoughtfully, "He does, Andre. Indeed, He does."

Roland then expressed the concern that had been building in his mind since they first recruited Landro almost three years before. How could they protect themselves against unfit candidates?

"We now have practical and strategic considerations, Andre. Secrecy protects us—yes—but it also poses a problem. We must find a way to ensure that the new people we bring here are truly worthy and committed to the Great Work . . . and that, once accepted among us, they'll be forever bound to us in secrecy."

"What do you have in mind? An oath of some kind?"

"An oath, yes. But more. We need something to make sure they will not turn back in moments of spiritual weakness—or, for the less honorable, betray us and reveal our beliefs and activities."

"Is such protection possible?"

"I don't know. But I have given much thought to an idea. The Cathar hatred of the crucifix provided me the key. We agree that veneration of the cross as an instrument of torture is abhorrent to our teachings, do we not?"

"Yes of course we do."

"What if we test our new members by having them violate the crucifix in a solemn ritual—to trample into the ground the very symbol of vicarious blood sacrifice?"

Andre was horrified.

"Are you mad?"

"Remember, it is not Christ that we violate, Andre! It is the slave religion that has been built in his name."

"Moments ago you spoke of your concerns for our immortal souls and those of our students. Now I understand why!"

"He who takes one step upon this path must arrive inevitably at the end thereof."

Andre laughed as he noted, "Such a ritual would certainly be of help if we brought in the wrong person. If he were interrogated and admitted to trampling the crucifix, he would know his life was forfeit."

"Welcome, my friend, to the point of no return."

Roland said nothing more, but his face registered increasing tension and determination. Then, suddenly, "In the name of all that is Holy, I proclaim myself free of the false symbols of my birth!"

Roland pulled the crucifix from his neck, flung it on the ground, and forcefully stamped it underfoot.

Andre looked on, his hands trembling with passion. He removed his own crucifix and threw it on the ground next to Roland's.

"I, too, reject the faith of my birth! It is by reviling Error that we make ourselves worthy to love Truth."

Andre trampled his crucifix.

The two Templars looked at each other, deeply cognizant of the irrevocable step they had taken.

"Inform the men we assemble here tomorrow night."

CHAPTER 50

The group of Templars stood in the torch-lit cavern the following night. All were wearing the full regalia of the Order as they listened to Roland. His voice resonated in the vastness of the cave.

"My Brothers, fellow seekers of the Light Within. We have been drawn together by our mutual desire for Pure Wisdom. Our bonds have allowed us to progress as students of the Great Work of liberation. Yet today we stand at a crossroads.

"Until now, we have spoken and studied as friends. We have explored doctrines and techniques that have led each of us to deeper self-knowledge. Yet danger threatens as suspicions against us grow.

"To continue further, we must pledge ourselves anew. Should anyone not be prepared for such a commitment, now is the time to withdraw."

He paused. The men all stared at him with greater concentration.

"As we continue on this path, we will attract others. The Light is ever expanding and cannot be contained.

"In time, our duties in the Order will of necessity separate us into many different countries. As we travel, each of us will come upon worthy candidates in search of Light. To him who is ready, the teacher appears and each of you may one day be that teacher.

"Yet there will be the ever-present danger of spies and even traitors in our midst. We will need to protect ourselves against such enemies.

"Therefore we intend to swear ourselves to certain obligations with a ceremony that each of you will repeat with those whom you find worthy."

Andre spoke up.

"Are you willing to take upon yourselves these greater burdens?"

They replied in unison, "We are."

Roland continued, "These oaths will remain indelible marks upon your souls. They will be eternally branded upon your very essence.

"You will be forever compromised among your fellows. Each of us will witness your actions here. If you are discovered, or betray us, you will face trial and execution before the civil and religious authorities.

"Therefore, one last time I warn you. If you persist, you are bound to remain. Do you choose to continue?"

Each knight nodded in affirmation as Roland made eye contact with him.

"Then you will repeat after me. Begin by stating your names, individually in succession."

He began, "I, Roland de Provence . . ."

"I, Andre d'Avignon . . ."

"I, Landro de Villiers . . ."

"I, Robert of York . . ."

"I, Rene d'Anjou . . ."

"I, Fernando Ramirez . . ."

Now the men, as one, following Roland's lead, repeated the oath of the Templar Inner Circle.

". . . declare myself a Soldier of the Light, a servant of Universal Truth.

"I swear to follow Truth no matter where may it lead,

"and to build my life upon the Truth I discover.

"I swear to seek the Light Within—to grow in wisdom and spiritual power,

"to discover and accomplish my true purpose in life,

"and to do battle for the emancipation of the human race from dogma and superstition.

"I swear eternal secrecy and protection of my brothers, and will regard their safety as my own."

The torches seemed to flicker as the oath-taking continued.

"Further, I affirm that I am a divine being in a physical body.

"As the essence of God is present in my flesh, I renounce Original Sin as a lie."

As the meaning of these words became clear, some of the men began to shift about. The renunciation of Original Sin was heresy. But the group remained resolute and continued.

"I reject all intercessors between God and Man.

"I accept responsibility for my own life.

"I declare that as a Man of Honor I refuse to allow an innocent person to suffer in my place.

"Thus, I despise the crucifix as a symbol of spiritual deception."

Rapid glances were exchanged. Some averted their eyes. Others, such as Landro, showed by the firm set of their faces an air of utter seriousness and exaltation.

"I therefore place my foot upon this cross to show my contempt for such a false symbol and the cowardice it implies."

Andre uncovered the large crucifix that had lain unseen on the floor of the cavern throughout the oath-taking. Beginning with Roland, each man in turn approached and trampled it underfoot. A mixture of horror and liberation was present in each one of them.

Roland proceeded with the ceremony.

"You will now remove your garments, carrying only your white tunic with you."

The Templars uneasily removed their mantles, chain mail, tunics, and underclothing. Roland led the naked warriors through a tunnel and into a secondary cavern that contained an altar.

On the altar sat the Golden Head flanked by a single candlestick. Around the head lay a pile of black cords. The torchlight reflected on the head in an eerie mix of light and shadow.

"I now hand each of you a cord. You will wrap it around your waist and tie it with a strong knot. From this day forward it will encircle you under your tunic, reminding you of the solemn oaths you have sworn and of the unbreakable bonds we have formed with each other."

The Templars tied the cords around their waists, then put on their tunics again.

"This is the sacred Head of one who led the way. One who succeeded in experiencing unity with divinity. This is Baphomet, the Father of Understanding, our true Grand Master, Hasan *ala dhikri as salaam*. We are irrevocably tied to him, just as these cords bind each of us to the other."

Roland stopped and looked at his fellow initiates.

"You are now sanctified. Go forth, my Brothers, and spread the Light."

They bestowed the Kiss of Peace, each on the other, as a gesture of unity and solidarity.

Sinan sat in meditation in his private chamber at Al-Kaph. Dressed in his white robe, the Master gazed through his mind's eye with satisfaction upon the far away scene in the cavern of initiation. Aisha sat cross-legged in front of him. They opened their eyes together.

Sinan spoke quietly, "It is done."

CHAPTER 51

Several days later, Guillaume was bursting with energy as Gaston de Navarre entered the room. Alerted that a significant development had occurred, Guillaume exclaimed, "Report!"

"Jean d'Evreux, one of the younger Templars, has been observed in lengthy conversation with Roland on three occasions."

"Have they been overheard?"

"No, Commander. They seem to have gone out of their way to prevent it."

Guillaume considered his options. Jean was a recent recruit. His youth and inexperience would make him vulnerable. Perhaps this would finally be Guillaume's chance to shed light on the dark undercurrents he knew were swirling around Acre.

"Bring him before me. A ruse might pry the truth from his lips."

Gaston left to fetch Jean. Guillaume paced around his office, becoming increasingly flushed and agitated. An apprehensive Jean d'Evreux, just twenty-years-old, was brought in by Gaston and two sergeants. The three of them left the room and waited outside as Guillaume proceeded alone with Jean.

Pounding his fist on the desk, Guillaume was direct.

"You are, I submit, a traitor and a heretic!"

His words were sudden, raw, and angry. Jean was visibly shaken by this unexpected accusation.

"You have listened to heresy, and worse, have returned to hear more!"

Grabbing a random sheaf of papers, he shook them in Jean's face.

"I have extensive evidence of your heretical and treasonous activities—including verbatim reports of conversations.

"You have two choices: You can confess your sins voluntarily—in which case I will advocate leniency before the Grand Master.

Or, should you refuse to cooperate, you will be examined, tortured, and placed on trial for your life."

Jean was shaking.

"I have no knowledge of any of this! Please believe me!"

Guillaume—his temper at a flash point—summoned the guards back into the room and Jean was dragged off to the dungeon.

The dark and clammy air in the room below the castle seemed to reek with an aura of the fear and pain its victims had left behind.

A guard placed a burning hot iron on Jean's chest. The hiss of broiling flesh was mixed with Jean's screams of agony.

Guillaume was enraged and shouted out.

"Better a searing of the flesh than eternal torment in the fires of Hell!"

The horror continued as the pathetic young warrior was beaten and scourged, and further burned on various parts of his body. Finally Jean's face revealed a look of utter terror as a glowing iron poker moved toward his eyes. As he felt its heat, he cried out in desperation.

"Stop! Stop! I'll tell you whatever you want! Anything! Anything!"

The interrogation moved back to Guillaume's office. A Templar scribe was writing down Jean's confession. Jean was shaking, haggard, utterly miserable, and broken. They had covered his burns with rags. He sobbed as he spoke.

"I felt far from God. I confided in Roland."

Guillaume asked, "Where did this take place?"

"On patrol. We were camped near Safed for the night."

"How did he respond?"

"He said that he himself once felt such pain, and that he would speak of it with me. But first I must swear an oath to hold secret all that he said."

"Did you swear such an oath?"

Jean looked down in shame. "I did."

"Then what did he say?"

"He said that separation from God is an illusion—that the angry God of the scriptures is a myth."

"Did you dispute this blasphemy?"

"I did. I said that God is angry because of our sins—that He withdraws His presence from us because we transgress His laws."

"And?"

"Roland said that each man must act according to what he personally judges to be right—not what priests tell him is right."

Guillaume fumed, "This is folly! Man is born with sin on his soul! How shall a man know right from wrong, except by God's law?"

"Roland denies that we are born evil! He says that we are divine creatures—that there is a flame that burns in every heart of man!"

"Blasphemy!"

Guillaume was pacing in a frenzy of emotion. He had known such heresies would infect the Order since the day King Henry allowed Roland to remain behind at Al-Kaph with the Saracen barbarians. And here, at last, was the absolute confirmation.

"If each man decided for himself what's right and wrong, men would be ruled by their appetites, indulging every whim and passion. Chaos would rule!"

"Roland said that individual freedom is not in conflict with cooperation and the common happiness. A man who follows his true purpose in life is never in conflict with the true purpose of others."

"And how is man to discover this so-called 'true purpose'?"

"Roland said that a man can look inside himself, discover his divine nature, and be changed."

"Witchcraft!

Guillaume's anger was palpable. He pointed to the scribe.

"Are you getting this?"

The scribe nodded in agreement and caught Guillaume's eye in recognition of the heresies they were uncovering.

Guillaume continued with Jean.

"What does he say of the Holy Scriptures that condemn such sorceries? Does he not submit to the authority of God's revealed Word?"

"He says that a book is not true just because it says it is true—or because we've been raised to believe it is true."

"Is there no end to this? Did he not fear that you would report him? An oath to a heretic is of no effect."

"In my weakness, I saw truth in his words. He sensed my agreement. No matter—it would be my word against his. We were alone."

"What does he say of faith?"

"He told me faith is unnecessary. A man of wisdom begins by doubting—by challenging everything. A man must believe nothing until he finds it out for himself."

"Finds out how?"

"By his own experience, and by reason."

Guillaume scoffed.

"He claims experience of God?"

"He does."

"He is mad! He is surely in the bonds of Satan."

"He calls Satan a childish superstition. And he denies Hell. He says it's blasphemy to charge God with such cruelty."

Guillaume shouted, "He serves Satan!"

Then he pivoted to what he hoped would be a different line of inquiry.

"Who else believes as he does? How many others have joined his foul company?"

"I do not know—truly! I have spoken only with him. He said nothing of anyone else."

"Yes, Roland is clever. It is indeed your word against his. How shall we know the truth of your confession? The penalty for false accusation against a Brother is severe."

Jean grasped for a response that could satisfy the crazed Guillaume. Finally, a memory came to him and his eyes lit up with hope.

"Wait! Roland no longer wears a crucifix around his neck. He wears a strange black cord tied about his waist."

Guillaume was riveted by Jean's words.

Jean described being on patrol with Roland. The Templars were attacked by a Saracen band near Sepphoris.

"Roland was wounded by a saber. That night, as the wound on his side was stitched up by torchlight, I caught a glimpse of the black cord."

Guillaume was elated. At last he had the proof he so desperately needed.

"I have seen such a cord before."

He thought back to his foiled interrogation of the Assassin spy. He saw again the black cord tied around the waist of the Infidel, and the exchange of glances of recognition and sympathy between Tafir and Roland.

Guillaume called for the guards.

"Detain this man until his allegations are verified."

He then spoke to Jean in a calmer tone.

"Your wounds will be tended to. You will be relieved of your Templar regalia and expelled from the Order. You will be allowed to join the Cistercians for the sake of your soul."

Then he bellowed out further orders to another of the guards.

"Ready my armor! Assemble the men! We ride to arrest a heretic and a traitor. He camps with a detachment west of Tiberias."

CHAPTER 52

Roland and several other Templars were sitting around a camp-fire, staring at the glowing embers and talking together. Andre was not present.

The soldiers, alerted by the sound of approaching hoof beats, reached for their weapons and rose. Moments later, a Templar detachment entered the camp. Guillaume rode forward to confront Roland.

"The game is up, my friend! You stand accused of heresy and witchcraft!"

He ordered the sergeants. "Seize him!"

Two sergeants dismounted and pinned Roland's arms behind his back. He did not resist. Guillaume stepped forward, unsheathed his dagger and cut open Roland's tunic to his waist. A torch was brought close, revealing the absence of a crucifix around his neck and the presence of the incriminating cord around his waist. Roland showed no sign of fear.

"Friends of Saracens are traitors to Christ!"

Guillaume produced a crucifix.

"Kiss the cross of your Savior!"

Roland squared his shoulders with defiance and refused to comply. Their eyes were locked in open warfare.

"Take him away!"

Roland was placed in custody without having spoken a word.

PART NINE

THE ALBIGENSIAN CRUSADES

CHAPTER 53

The sound of hammers resounded outside Guillaume's office window as a gallows was being built in the courtyard below. A knock on the door was followed by the entrance of a guard apologizing for the intrusion.

"Excuse me, sir. A messenger."

"Send him in."

As the messenger entered, Guillaume impatiently spoke up, "Report."

"News from France, Commander. The papal envoy Pierre de Castelnau has been murdered by suspected agents of Raymond, Count of Toulouse, a known abettor of the Cathar heretics.

"The Holy Father has ordered an immediate crusade against the Cathars of Languedoc to extirpate their heresy once and for all. He offers the lands of the heretics to any French nobles who will join the fight.

"I am ordered to convey the following instructions to you: You are to report to the Abbot of Citeaux who has been placed in charge of the operation."

The messenger handed Guillaume a pouch. Guillaume opened it, withdrew the dispatch, broke open the seal, and read.

He replied, "I will depart within the week. Before I deal with the Cathar heretics, I must first take care of one of my own!"

CHAPTER 54

Faint movements registered in the bushes near the moat of the Templar fortress. The moonlight shone on the castle silhouetting it against the night sky. A half-dozen individuals, clad in tight-fitting, hooded black outfits, slipped quietly into the water and swam to the base of the citadel. They then carefully and methodically climbed its walls, using the irregularities of the stones and masonry for hand- and footholds.

Once inside, the team flowed silently through the hallways of the castle. The members of the elite unit made piercing eye contact when they encountered Templar sentinels, vibrating a mysterious sound whose unearthly pitch shuttered the consciousness of each guard. The sentries were thus lulled into a hypnotic state. The intruders were as phantoms, gliding through the folds of a mist of invisibility and unreality as they made their way to Roland's cell.

Roland was in chains, seated in deep meditation. He was roused by the sound of his jailer opening the cell door and stepping inside, carrying a large ring of iron keys. The guard moved mechanically, as if his will had been overpowered and he was in a trance. Roland noted six hooded figures slipping in behind him and closing the door.

One of the black-clad warriors gestured for the guard to unlock Roland's shackles. The jailer was then rendered unconscious by a firm squeeze to his throat and the vibrating of the otherworldly tone into his ear. He was gently guided down as he collapsed to the floor.

As the team members removed their hoods, Aisha stood before Roland.

He looked up in utter astonishment.

"Aisha! My God! Is it really you?"

"Roland! *Alhamdulillah!* You are safe. We are in time."

She lowered her voice, "Is the Golden Head protected?"

"Yes," he whispered. "It is in Andre's care."

Aisha looked deep into Roland's eyes. As she moved closer, she sensed his reserve.

"You have a woman."

"I have a wife in France."

"You love her very much?"

"We are as one soul in two bodies."

This was news she did not expect.

"So now you will go to her."

After a moment's hesitation, she explained his escape route.

"A camel, a bundle of Arab clothing, and a bag of dinars await you in the trees beyond the moat. Disguise yourself, travel southward. You can catch a northbound ship for Genoa or Marseilles."

Aisha put a talisman with magic writing around his neck.

"I prepared this myself. It is charged with strong magic to keep you safe."

Roland clutched the token of her love. They regarded each other in silence. His voice was filled with great sadness.

"What has been the purpose of all this? My running away now means our mission is a failure. There are men here eager to learn."

"Another will take your place. The Golden Chain stretches to Infinity."

"Andre has grown rapidly, but he needs more time."

Aisha looked at him with confidence.

"He will be ready."

She then explained the new parameters of Roland's continuing mission.

"Your work here is complete, my Brother. You must now carry this Wisdom to Europe, the land of your birth, and there teach new people what it means to live in the Light."

"Will I see you again?"

Aisha spoke sadly and melodiously.

"We shall rise together through the spheres, in dreams and in visions."

She gazed into his eyes, then turned abruptly and addressed one of the Assassins in Arabic.

"*RooH halla!* [Go now!]"

The group went forth, escorting Roland from the cell as Aisha looked on.

Aisha moved quickly through the halls of the stronghold to Andre's bed chamber. She found the young warrior asleep on a simple pallet. The features of his face were visible by the dim light of a single candle. Aisha silently approached his sleeping form. She knelt by his head, looked heavenward, and threw her arms out at her sides at shoulder level.

An intensifying radiance surrounded her. The light continued to build until she brought her hands together on her forehead to form the upright Sign of Fire. The radiance coalesced within the glowing triangle. Then she looked down at Andre, straightened her arms, and placed the triangle of her hands directly in front of his forehead. A powerful blaze of light filled the area on Andre's brow, energizing and then awakening his third-eye chakra.

While his physical body remained asleep, Andre's astral form, clothed in a white robe, arose and stood facing Aisha in a space filled with emptiness. A current of energy passed between them, emanating at first from Aisha but then returned with increasing focus by Andre. They remained staring into each other's eyes.

When his chakra awakening and their astral exchange were completed, Aisha put her attention to the physical task at hand. She untied the black cord from around his waist. She then carefully hung a crucifix from his neck. When all was complete, she left the still-sleeping Andre as silently as she had come in.

Outside the castle by the moat, Roland hurriedly donned a djellaba, mounted the waiting camel, and made his escape.

CHAPTER 55

The next morning chaos reigned throughout the Templar headquarters. There was a frenzy of activity as soldiers were rushing
back and forth in the courtyard. Various officers shouted a bar-
rage of orders as men hurriedly finished dressing and ran to their
horses to saddle up.

Andre emerged from the dormitory, puzzled by the frenzy
of motion all about him. He walked up to a knight standing in
the courtyard.

"What's going on?"

"Roland has escaped."

Andre showed a look of complete surprise, mingled with
quiet glee.

"When? How?"

"Sometime after midnight. The guards were set upon and
overcome by men dressed in black."

Andre was astonished.

"Here, in the fortress? How is that possible?"

"They were not seen by the sentries, either coming or going."

Another knight spoke up, "It was witchcraft!"

The first man continued to fill Andre in on the emerging
details.

"Guillaume is sending out patrols to recapture him."

As the three men talked, a sergeant approached and spoke
directly to Andre.

"You are ordered to report to Guillaume immediately."

Andre entered the commander's office. He found Guillaume
studying a map, looking irritated with frustration and rage
showing on his face. He glanced up as Andre walked in. His eyes
were of flaming granite.

Andre's demeanor was more confident than normal. He bore
the aura of a leader—focused and self-assured. Aisha's energy

awakening had touched a hitherto passive portion of his mind and given him access to previously dormant capabilities.

Guillaume stated the obvious, "You've heard what has happened, of course. You are known to be his closest friend."

Andre was not intimidated.

"What are you implying, sir?"

"I imply nothing. There is no evidence against you. Any natural suspicion that might—rightly or wrongly—be directed toward you can easily be dispelled."

Guillaume spoke in a firm tone, "You will undo your tunic and mail, and stand before me unclothed from the waist up."

"Sir?"

"It's a simple command. You will recall your oath of obedience."

Guillaume's expression revealed an air of triumph and anticipation. Andre complied boldly and without flinching. He was fully prepared to face the consequences of his firmly held beliefs. He knew he would be exposed when Guillaume discovered Andre's black cord and the absence of a crucifix.

Andre grew incredulous as he removed his linen shirt and realized the black cord was no longer tied around his waist and that a proper Templar crucifix hung from his neck. Guillaume's face fell in disappointment.

The commander composed himself.

"Thank you. Reassume your armor."

After a moment he continued.

"Andre d'Avignon, you are relieved of your command."

Andre replied forcefully, "Sir, on what grounds?"

"You leave with me for France within the week. You will assume a new command once we arrive there. The Holy Father needs battle-hardened knights to exterminate the Cathar heresy and bring righteousness and peace to that demon-ridden land."

Andre listened with a complete sense of unreality.

✝ ✝ ✝

Still in a state of disbelief, Andre emerged from Guillaume's office and out of the castle into the courtyard. He observed mounted patrols still riding out through the gate. As he moved toward his own horse, he encountered fellow initiate Rene d'Anjou mounting up nearby.

"I am ordered to France—within the week," Andre said in a lowered voice.

Rene was stunned, "How can this be? We are left alone!"

"I will return when I can. Until then, you have each other."

Rene was in despair.

"The Light will fade from this land."

"You are the Light! Inform the others. Let us gather again at the cavern tomorrow evening. You will all simply continue your training and work in my absence. And by God's grace, I will return before long."

They grasped each other's forearms in solidarity.

"Remember this: great power is released from deep inside you when you push beyond what you think are your limits."

He then smiled as he quipped, "Come, we must appear to look for Roland."

CHAPTER 56

Andre looked out across the harbor as the blue-white ripples of the Mediterranean glistened in the sun. A Templar ship was being loaded; its sails unfurled. Knights were preparing to board for the voyage to France. Guillaume stood near the ramp barking out orders.

Native women—some carrying baskets of food, others with rich fabrics draped over their arms—made a last attempt to sell their wares to the departing Templars.

An old woman, bent with age, approached Andre and feebly extended her arm, which was draped with a colorful embroidered shawl. He took a quick glance and signaled no with his hand. She pulled the shawl from her arm with her other hand and held it out toward him anyway:

"*Tfaddal.* [Please take this.]"

"*RooHi halla.* [Go away, now.]"

"*Ittalla' alayi.* [Look at me.]"

"*Muta-assef. Ma biddi yah.* [I'm sorry. I don't want it.]"

The old woman whispered, "*Sallmili 'ala sayyed Roland.* [Remember me to Roland.]"

Stunned, Andre looked into her eyes and suddenly recalled the enticing young woman he had seen for the first time in the banquet room at Al-Kaph years before. He realized the figure before him was Aisha in disguise.

Her soft eyes were bright with tears. She pushed the shawl into his hands, turned quickly, and hurried away.

Andre felt the fabric of the shawl and noticed that something was wrapped inside. He looked down, unfolded it, and found his black cord.

As he watched the receding figure of Aisha disappear into the crowd, a fellow Templar called out to him to board.

The Templar ship cut through the water enjoying good sailing winds. Andre and Guillaume stood on deck, surveying the vast Mediterranean panorama while lost in their own thoughts. Separated by age and temperament, two more different people might be hard to find. Yet they were bound together by more than either realized. Both had been raised as only-children and had since lost their families. When their ship landed in the European homeland, they would each be alone, wanderers, whose long absence in the Holy Land was less onerous than it was for many of their fellows. The Templar Order provided them family as it offered opportunity for comradeship.

On the deck of an Arab dhow, Roland, dressed in Arab garb, looked down at Aisha's talisman and then across the sea toward the horizon.

CHAPTER 57

Simon and Arianne's home in the ancient town of Albi sat on a nicely tended lot near the bank of the River Tarn. Located in the neighborhood of Castelviel, it was not far from the Church of Saint-Salvi.

They had returned from their long stay in Avignon and were in conversation during the afternoon meal. Arianne was giving voice to her deep concerns.

"There has been no word from him for many months. I fear for his safety."

Simon countered, "He must be cautious under the circumstances. I'm sure he is well, my child."

As they spoke, a messenger arrived on horseback with a letter for Simon. He opened it and read.

"It's from Citeaux. I am informed that our old friend the abbot and papal legate Arnaud Amaury will arrive in three days to confer with me about the 'serious situation' we face."

"Is that bee buzzing around again?"

"This time, I fear, he means to sting."

At the appointed time, the papal legate Arnaud Amaury arrived with his guard, which included Guillaume and Andre. Simon greeted the abbot and ushered him inside. Arnaud, in his fifties, was painfully thin and stooped yet with a burning fire in his eyes.

The rest of the party remained outside tending to their horses and talking among themselves while awaiting the abbot.

In the sitting room of Simon's house, refreshments were brought in for Amaury. Then the two men got down to the business at hand.

The legate spoke first. His thin and bloodless lips arranged themselves into a twisted and insincere smile as he attempted to sound conciliatory and rational.

"You know why I'm here. The Holy Father is a man of infinite patience. He offers yet another opportunity for you to see reason. You have great influence among the people in this region. It's no secret that the armies of the north even now prepare to descend upon your cities. I do not wish to see bloodshed."

"We also condemn warfare."

"Alas, this is an age of crusades. It's the nature of things. Men are impatient; they prefer actions rather than words. Surely you understand this."

"They use religion for political ends. Surely I understand that!"

Arnaud recoiled slightly.

"This can all be avoided. Friend, the Holy Father would understand why you remain so obstinate?"

"We strive to be *katharos*—pure. In that, surely obstinacy is a virtue?"

"But you imply that the Mother Church is impure."

"We do not simply imply it; we assert it! You have become a church of wolves, intoxicated with wealth and power. Jesus preached simplicity and frugality. He preached rejection of this world. The pope is the richest man in Europe! You must abandon either your luxury or your preaching."

Anger was growing in Arnaud but he fought to restrain himself. He stood up to relieve the rising tension.

"The Scriptures tell us that wise King Solomon was a man of wealth and power. He built a Temple to the Lord, using a vast fortune of gold and silver far exceeding anything we have in Rome."

"And what became of Solomon? His heart became proud; he abandoned himself to pleasures; he took wives and concubines by the hundreds; he forgot God. And now the Roman Church follows his example. Matthew reminds us that, 'Where your treasure is, there will your heart be also.'"

"You do the Church an injustice."

Simon spoke softly, "Our places of worship are the fields and forests and our simple homes. Where do you think God is more likely to reveal Himself?"

"Yet salvation is possible only through the sacraments of the Church. Man cannot approach God except through the successors of St. Peter."

"Ah, now we come to the crux of the matter! We declare that any person can approach the divine. Man has no need of intercessors. A man has only to look within his heart to find the kingdom of God."

Arnaud bristled. "Does not Isaiah warn us of the danger of such spiritual pride? 'Woe unto them that are wise in their own eyes, and prudent in their own sight.'"

"No! We Cathars seek first the kingdom of God. We strengthen the inner spirit by prayer, contemplation, fasting, and abstaining from earthly temptations. We seek to purge our souls from the dross of earth; to reunite with our celestial identity. We do not need the Church's permission to do this."

As Simon and the legate continued their conversation, the guards were milling about in the front yard. Arianne approached Guillaume.

"Sir, I am Arianne d'Albi, daughter of Simon. Do your men require food or refreshment? It is freely offered."

Guillaume replied perfunctorily, "I am Guillaume de Gonneville. I ask only water for my men and their horses, my lady."

Guillaume looked admiringly at Arianne, finding her disturbingly attractive. His eyes glinted with pure masculine interest. Guillaume had spent decades in the near-monastic Templar environment. He was unfamiliar with and uncomfortable in the presence of women. This one in particular seemed to stimulate a dark and mysterious lust in him. He found these powerful feelings vexing and alarming.

Arianne sensed his thoughts and was on guard.

"I see you're a Templar, sir. Many Templars were born in this region."

"And now they return to assist the French lords in restoring the True Faith to this land."

"I fear the French lords are more interested in our lands than our faith."

"They are good Christians who follow the orders of the Holy Father. In any case, my lady, it is no business of yours."

Arianne was unfazed by such rudeness.

"You believe a woman should not concern herself with matters of politics and religion?"

"The Templar Rule advises that the company of women is a dangerous thing, for by it the Devil has led many from the straight path."

Arianne, in mock alarm, asked, "'Dangerous'? Shall you summon the guards?"

The ill-tempered Guillaume replied curtly, "Return to your embroidery, my lady, and hold your tongue. We will speak no further. I pray that you and your miserable land will be healed of the filthy contagion so clearly in evidence here!"

Arianne got in the last word as Guillaume stalked off, "If the prayers of dogs were answered, bones would rain from the sky!"

Andre observed the exchange from a distance. After Guillaume left Arianne, Andre, leading his horse, timed his gait to intercept her as she approached the door of the house. He bent down, appearing to examine the horse's hoof. As Arianne passed, he spoke in a low voice.

"Don't turn around. I'm Roland's friend Andre. Say nothing. Just listen."

Arianne stopped, facing away from him and pretending to adjust the band in her hair.

"Roland was arrested by Guillaume on a charge of heresy. He was scheduled to be executed but escaped. He may be on his way here. If he shows up, you must warn him that Guillaume is in France and will pursue him through the gates of Hell if necessary. Tell him, please, that he must be careful."

Arianne turned pale. She resumed walking without looking back.

Inside the house, the trays were nearly empty. Simon and Arnaud were both seated again. The debate continued.

Arnaud explained the Church's position—that no Christian has the option to practice his faith without recognizing the pope.

"The authority of the Church derives from Christ and the apostles. The vicars of Christ must be obeyed for the good of all. We teach the proper ways to live and to worship, to serve God and the State, and how to maintain harmonious relationships with your fellow man."

"Beware the man who exercises authority under the guise of preserving order! Harmony is the noble cloak that men drape over their will to power."

Arnaud gestured toward the walls of the room.

"I see no crucifix here. What of it?"

"A false symbol! You venerate an instrument of torture. Christ did not die for our sins. He lived to show us the way to God."

Arnaud asked, "Does that 'way' involve the repudiation of the holy sacraments? Does that 'way' permit women to preach? It's said your own daughter ministers to the people."

Simon replied, "The form of one's physical body is irrelevant. All souls are equally divine. Is it so grievous a crime to treat women as equals?"

"In attempting to reform the Church, you create your own perversions. Your heresy is deliberate and obstinate. To resist the Church is to resist God!"

Simon's frustration mounted.

"Do you not find it ironic that your Church was built on the foundation of the very disciple who denied Christ three times? We need not apologize for our worship. This is an argument that has no resolution."

"Oh, it has a resolution—the censure of excommunication."

"Is a duck to be threatened by being cast into the river?"

"You forget our armies!"

"To be persecuted and killed as the apostles and martyrs of old? Is that such a horrible fate? The divine within me rejoices."

The legate rose angrily. He was finished.

"This land shall be purged!"

Arnaud stormed out. Arianne walked into the sitting room from the kitchen where she had been listening to the last part of their conversation.

Simon looked up, "So much for 'infinite patience.'"

CHAPTER 58

When Roland's boat reached the island of Cyprus, he discarded his Arab dress and assumed the air of a French merchant. Some four weeks later, he arrived at the port of Marseilles and disembarked from the lateen-rigged commercial ship on which he had booked passage. He then walked to a nearby corral and purchased a horse for the journey through the Languedoc.

After a circuitous route with a number of stops along the way, he at last arrived in Albi. He boarded his horse at a local stable and continued on foot toward Simon's house. In a small alley along the way, he changed his garb once again—the outlaw now appearing as an elderly peasant in tattered rags, bent forward on a cane.

He shuffled toward the door of Simon's house. He knocked and Arianne answered. Looking down and disguising his voice, Roland pleaded, "Alms, my lady?"

Arianne regarded the pitiful figure in front of her, invited him into the vestibule, then turned and called toward the kitchen, "Bring what's left of the fish, Marguerite. And Henri's old coat."

Arianne regarded the old man's tattered cloak.

"You are in need of something better against the evening chill, I think."

In his own voice, Roland answered, "Once I was told that a horse of good breed is not dishonored by his saddle."

Arianne was stunned; then sunshine broke across her face. She rushed to him. He straightened up and held out his arms. They embraced and kissed.

"My love, I have looked for you every day for months. Andre said you would come."

Roland was surprised, "Andre?"

"He was here, in the guard of the papal legate Arnaud Amaury. Guillaume was part of the guard too."

"Guillaume!"

"You are branded a heretic and traitor. Andre told me to warn you that if Guillaume learns you're in France, he'll leave no stone unturned until you're found. It is not safe for you here."

Ominously Roland answered, "It's not safe for anyone."

Later that night Simon, Arianne, and Roland sat together deep in conversation. Arianne wore a new necklace, a gift from Roland. Its pendant was a white dove pointing downward, its wings spread in flight. The three companions were basking in the joy of their reunion, the aftereffects of an excellent meal, and the time spent filling each other in on their last several months of activity.

Finally the conversation turned to the present situation in southern France and the anticipated papal invasion.

Roland began with a report of the intelligence he had ascertained on his journey from Marseilles.

"The armies that assembled in Lyon in June have marched south along the Rhone then into the Languedoc. Amaury leads the Crusade as the pope's representative. He has set up his headquarters at Montpellier. The northern nobleman Simon de Montfort commands the military. Attacks are imminent. Béziers may be first."

Simon was concerned by this news.

"My sister Iolande lives in Béziers! I must go to her. I must stand with her at the end."

"It's not the end yet. There's much sympathy for the Cathar cause. Many of your neighbors see truth in your ways. And many Templars find it repugnant to set their swords against fellow Christians. They will not join the French lords. The Templar Grand Master himself has said there is only one true Crusade—the Crusade against the Saracens. At the least, many Templars will remain neutral; and some will fight for you."

Arianne was grateful to learn this.

"This is the first we have heard of allies."

"One of the initiates of our circle was injured in battle. He was sent here to France to command a Templar house in Collioure. I met with him last week. He makes plans to shelter Cathars in his province and to evacuate as many as possible by sea.

"Other Templars prepare to take refugees into their preceptories. Some commanders are even accepting Cathars into their ranks—which will give them immunity from prosecution."

Arianne asked, "What of your father, Count Bertram?"

"I have also visited him. He has quietly liquidated much of his wealth and is financing mercenaries to defend the province."

Simon spoke up in a pained tone, "But we believe that the taking of life is wrong."

Roland replied firmly, "Shall evil then win by default? Shall we play the part of passive lambs being led meekly to our deaths? I believe we must fight against the forces of tyranny and oppression. We must defend our right to live and worship as we choose."

After their conversation concluded, Simon went off to bed. Roland and Arianne sat in silence with each other for a time. Feeling the need for some air, they got up and went outside. It was a beautiful night; the cool air played off their skin. They walked into the nearby wooded park under a sky bright with stars. In the intimacy of the darkness, they strolled in silence, savoring the joy of being together again.

Despite her lover's presence, Arianne was thoughtful and saddened.

"The world sinks deeper and deeper into darkness. The light grows faint . . . so faint."

Roland stopped walking, took her hands in his, and looked deeply into her eyes.

"Not the light of your eyes, Woman of my Heart."

"My chosen and preferred."

They kissed and stood close, her body pressing into his. A wind rose up and Roland draped his cloak over her shoulders. Thunder rumbled ominously in the distance. The sky darkened as clouds came forth to block the light of the stars. A storm was moving in.

CHAPTER 59

Mounted knights rode swiftly in procession through the French countryside. A stern-faced Guillaume led the group. From the rear, a knight on a white horse galloped up the ranks. The column slowed at his approach. The messenger was Andre. He shouted to Guillaume, "Orders from Commander de Montfort!"

"Yes?"

"We rendezvous with the counts of Nevers and Saint-Pol at Montagnac, then merge with the main force at Pinet. From there we advance to Béziers and take up a position east of the city."

Guillaume replied, "Inform the Under Marshal."

Andre answered, "Yes, sir."

Then Andre spoke up with hope in his voice to convey what he thought might be received as good news.

"There is talk that an accommodation may still be reached."

Guillaume flashed a look of disgust, then spurred his horse and rode on ahead.

CHAPTER 60

Back in Albi Roland, Arianne, and Simon were saddling their horses. Simon and Arianne gave final instructions to members of their household.

Roland tried again to convince his father-in-law to desist.

"Sir, I beg you to reconsider. Remain here in Albi. I will return from Béziers with your sister within three days."

"It's not for Iolande alone that I go to Béziers. There are hundreds of Cathar brethren there. Many may die in the coming battle. It is my duty and privilege to prepare them, and to stand with them."

"And mine," said Arianne.

Roland paused briefly, then realized he had no chance to dissuade them.

"So be it. We go together."

At Roland's father's estate, Count Bertram was overseeing continuing arrangements for the defense of his people and property in anticipation of the northern invasion. Children, pregnant women, the elderly, and infirm were being temporarily moved to secure locations out of harm's way. They were placed under the protection of some of the count's warriors, who were also charged with removing certain valuables and records in case the situation grew worse.

Simultaneously, storage facilities on the castle grounds were being checked and restocked as necessary with emergency provisions. Weapons were inventoried, organized, and assigned to those who would remain behind.

The great feudal estates of the day had been built around the lord's castle, a walled military fortress. The castle was surrounded by free peasants and bound serfs living in cottages and working the land. In times of great danger, these people left their homes and retreated behind the safety of the castle walls. Both armed attacks and general looting were not uncommon, but the nature of the coming threat was unique. A great sense of urgency motivated everyone.

A group of Templar knights rode into the courtyard to speak with Bertram.

"Greetings, your Excellency!"

"Welcome! What news?"

"The crusaders move faster than anticipated. Andre has sent word that Béziers is to be first. He will remain with his company and keep us informed as long as he's able."

Bertram asked, "What of the mission of Raymond-Roger de Trencavel? Has he seen Arnaud Amaury at Montpellier?"

"Amaury refused to receive him. Trencavel has returned to Carcassonne to organize his defenses."

Bertram was crestfallen.

"Then the die is cast. So we continue our preparations to take in refugees. How goes the equipping of the mountain retreats?"

"Supplied and provisioned."

"How are the houses of refuge?"

"In readiness."

"And the ships?"

The Templar answered, "The Provincial Master at Collioure is directing our maritime efforts."

"What is your strength?"

"Ninety-three mounted Templars ... plus six hundred mercenary knights—more than enough to handle de Montfort's reconnaissance troops."

"Use them wisely," Bertram cautioned.

"We'll keep ahead of the crusaders, and evacuate those Cathars we can. But there's little we can do for the people in Béziers."

Bertram answered ruefully, "Béziers. Its walls are strong. If they can hold out behind those walls for just a few weeks, their attackers may well lose interest in the rigors of maintaining a prolonged siege."

"May God grant them—and their walls—the strength and time they'll need!"

Bertram and the Templar leader grasped each other's forearms.

The Templars rode off and Bertram returned to directing the preparations. He knew there was no chance of withstanding a full military assault against his estate, but he was determined to hold out as long as possible. He would gather as much intelligence as he could about the intentions and vulnerabilities of the invaders.

CHAPTER 61

Roland, Arianne, and Simon traveled together on the sixty-mile journey from Albi to Béziers. The impressive city sat on a bluff above a river. It was protected by strong walls and many fortified towers and barbicans. As they entered a city gate, they found the town abuzz with activity.

They rode through the narrow, congested streets to the house of Iolande. She greeted her brother with an enthusiastic embrace.

"Simon! You should not have come here!"

"You knew I would come. You also know the Crusaders are readying their attack. Why have our brethren not left the city? The Crusader army is formidable."

"If we run, they win."

A group of Béziers fighters stood on the walkway of the city ramparts studying the scene below. The fields surrounding the town were filled with the assembled masses of Crusader forces. Thousands of fully armed and mounted knights were encamped with many thousands more foot soldiers, mercenaries, and camp followers.

Jacques, a young Catholic archer, was calculating distances and trajectories. He shook his head in astonishment.

"Look at this sea of soldiers! Unbelievable. Has all of France gone mad?"

His fellow townsman, Maurice, showed the same look of disbelief mixed with disgust. He reminded his companion of some of the reasons the recruiting efforts of the papal army had been so successful.

"The pope has offered full remission of sins to anyone who fights here for only forty days! Imagine that. To hell with penance. Just grab your traveling gear and walk or ride through the nice summer countryside until you reach an assembly of fellow cowards preparing to attack civilians."

Jacques was mortified, but mentioned the obvious.

"It is certainly easier and cheaper than struggling for months to reach the Holy Land where you'll need to fight against actual armed Infidels. The desert is far less inviting than the farm lands of the Languedoc!"

Maurice looked out again at the assembled mass below.

"Remember also that the pope has not only offered Cathar lands to these marauders, but the lands of any French nobles known to be Cathar supporters. That's almost all of them when you think of it. Our neighbors may be a little odd, but who hasn't benefited from their medical skills or their pleasant conversation?"

Jacques observed, "And for the foot soldiers, there's the promise of plunder that follows the battle. Imagine the stored treasures they will find for the looting if they can breach our walls."

Maurice looked again at the army below and spat in their direction.

"Let's make sure they don't! If we can hold out for even a month, most of the rabble will be on their way. Their forty days will be finished and their rotten souls will have been cleansed."

He spat over the wall again.

A mounted delegation led by the abbot-commander Arnaud Amaury approached the city walls under a flag of truce. He looked up at the battlements and addressed the representative of the city.

"The Holy Father requires your obedience. The Cathar heretics must be handed over."

The city spokesman replied, "It is not possible, my lord abbot."

"Do you dare refuse a direct command from the pope?"

"Our neighbors are guilty of no crime, yet you demand they be handed over. We are Christians, commanded by our Savior to practice love and tolerance."

"They are but a few hundred, in your city of thousands. Shall thousands suffer for the heresies of a few?"

"We are good Catholics, but we see godliness in these Cathars. They are our brothers and sisters. We shall not deliver them to the slaughter."

The legate screamed out in fury.

"Not slaughter—righteous judgment! We are the army of God!"

"Is God's army sent against the meek and poor-in-spirit?"

"You have one day to send them out! Comply, and your city will be spared. Consider carefully!"

The city spokesman answered with defiance.

"The blood of the innocent shall not be on our hands."

"Spare yourselves the fire of Hell!"

"Go to Hell—you and your 'army of God'!"

An enraged Amaury turned his horse abruptly and galloped off. His retinue followed as he tossed the banner of truce to the ground.

Amaury returned to the crusader forces outside the city walls and shook his head with loathing. Preparations were underway for the anticipated assault since the city leaders were firm in their determination not to capitulate before the superior force. The soldiers were dragging siege equipment toward the walls— including ladders, battering rams, siege hooks, and catapults.

Inside the walls the people of Béziers were also methodically preparing for the coming attack. Wood was placed beneath oil pots in preparation for boiling; archers stockpiled arrows in the towers and surveyed their field of fire; the gates were braced with large wooden beams. People attempted to place food supplies, water, and medicines within protected spaces and safe reach. Families discussed plans in the event of their being separated. Animals were locked in their pens with adequate food and water.

✝ ✝ ✝

After sunset, the frenetic pace of preparations had slowed. The Cathars of Béziers gathered in the torch-lit public square. People overflowed into the side streets. Simon walked out onto the small balcony of a building facing the square. As he raised his arms, the crowd fell silent.

"My brothers and sisters!

"It is with boundless joy and ecstasy that we come together tonight.

"Long ago we resolved to walk in the light of God. We are children of the Light—but sojourners in an evil world.

"Tonight, the forces of darkness close in around us.

"The hour approaches; yet we do not fear.

"The tempest draws nigh; yet we are not dismayed.

"False apostles, who pollute the word of Christ, seek our lives; yet we rejoice!"

As he looked out at his fellow Cathars, his heart was filled with love and admiration for their steadfastness.

"If death comes, is it such a dreadful thing? Death does not extinguish the flame that burns in our hearts. Death is our release from the bondage of flesh in this valley of sorrow.

"We must then bless our executioners as we forgive them.

"And we must thank our dear neighbors for their love and support, and for their courage.

"Let our own courage this day resound through the ages! Let us acquit ourselves like the divine spirits we are. Let us show the world how the righteous die.

"We are not alone. We leave this world together. And together we shall put on the garments of immortality and walk among the stars.

"There is nothing left to fear. Let us step bravely into eternity with joy and with gladness."

Simon paused and looked again upon those gathered before him.

"The hour is late. It is time for prayers and for rest. May the divine within you rejoice and be glad this night! Go in peace."

The people dispersed, talking among themselves. The mood was upbeat, if reflective.

Simon walked down the stairs of the building and out the door onto the street. A small child ran to his side, tugged on his tunic, and looked up at him.

"We are brave, Father."

CHAPTER 62

The next day was July 22, 1209. A group of armed warriors, after consultation with the burghers of the town council of Béziers, launched a surprise offensive against the invading army. Mounted knights poured out of a side gate of the city in a frenzied charge. Archers on the walls covered the sortie, raining arrows down on the crusader troops.

Opening the massive gates of the city by choice was a huge tactical blunder. The leaders of Béziers thus abandoned their sole source of defense against the mighty force assembled against them.

Amaury and Commander Simon de Montfort surveyed the scene from a distance. Simon was a thirty-five-year-old nobleman whose family estate was near Paris. De Montfort was known for his religious zeal, his military skills, and his ruthlessness.

Amaury was incredulous when he saw the warriors riding forth from Béziers.

"The fools are attacking!"

De Montfort hurriedly gave orders to an adjutant.

"Drive them back inside and pursue them closely. If we can get some men inside before the gate is closed—we have them!"

The abortive sortie was forced back into the city, closely pursued by an unruly band of foot soldiers and mercenaries who poured in through the gate. Once inside the walls of the city, the attackers quickly gained control and threw open the numerous gates to the main crusader forces.

De Montfort shouted, "They're in! Prepare to engage en masse!"

Trumpets sounded as the Crusaders converged on Béziers from all sides.

Iolande's house was far enough away from where the city wall was breached that she, Simon, and Arianne were yet unaware of the morning's catastrophic developments. They were engaged in bringing food and supplies up from the cellar, which was accessed by a hinged trapdoor in the floor.

As Simon emerged from below, he looked around the room and asked Arianne, "Where is my sister?"

"She just left to take some food to her friend Eleanor who is sick with fever."

"I asked her not to leave!"

At this moment Roland burst in, out of breath.

"The sortie has failed! The crusaders are inside the city walls!"

Simon exclaimed, "Iolande has gone to a friend's."

"I'll find her. Go into the cellar and wait. There is yet time before the fighting reaches this district."

Arianne directed him, "She's at the house next to the blacksmith, on the Rue Droite."

"We will go with you!" said Simon.

"It will be faster if I go alone. There's nothing more you can do now except keep Arianne safe. Please do this for me. I'll assess the movements of the troops and return with a plan."

Roland turned to Arianne and kissed her. Then he removed Aisha's talisman and hung it around Arianne's neck, saying under his breath, "*Aisha, deeri balek alayhaa.* [Aisha, keep her safe.]"

Roland helped father and daughter down the ladder into the cellar. Before closing the trapdoor, Roland handed his sword to Simon, hoping he would reconsider his pacifism if Arianne's life were threatened. Then he dashed into the street.

CHAPTER 63

Once inside the city, the Crusaders quickly gained control and began the bloody slaughter of Catholics and Cathars alike. Though the town held fewer than several hundred Cathars, Amaury later claimed to the pope that 20,000 people were put to the sword that day, essentially the entire population of Béziers. (This was surely an exaggeration as the city's population at the time of the massacre was closer to 14,000 souls.)

The Crusaders killed people in a frenzy. The mass murder of unarmed civilians included the sacking and looting of stores and homes as well as the random torching of occupied buildings. The violence degenerated into sheer madness with decapitations, rape, and torture. Children were thrown down wells and impaled on spears. Men were dragged behind horses. Fleeing citizens were used for target practice by the blood-intoxicated invaders. The town was drenched in gore and horror. The cries of the wounded rang through the air.

The violence of the crusading force during this first battle of the Albigensian Crusades was intended to serve notice to other cities in the region that resistance was futile.

Abbot-commander Arnaud Amaury directed the operations from horseback. A soldier ran up to him and shouted above the din.

"How are we to distinguish the Cathars from the Catholics?"

Fearing that Cathars might disguise themselves as Catholics and escape, Amaury replied, "Kill them all! God will know his own!"

Andre galloped down a city street in another part of town. Guillaume surreptitiously followed him. He had never trusted Andre and observed his current movements with curiosity. The Templar commander was afforded such luxury by the ruthless slaughter the army was conducting. The battle, such as it was, hardly demanded his personal participation since the civilian enemy was generally unable to mount any type of effective defense against even an unskilled footsoldier.

He watched as Andre shouted to a group of fleeing Cathars.

"Do you know Simon the Parfait? Does anyone know where he stays?"

Andre rode through the chaotic streets asking repeatedly after Simon. Finally a townsman answered, calling to him over the noise of the crowd. He pointed up a side street.

"He is at the house of his sister Iolande, off the Rue de la Portette near the ale house Lion Rouge."

Andre spurred his horse in the indicated direction.

Elsewhere, Béziers residents—Cathar and Catholic alike—retreated into the sanctuary of the Cathédrale Saint-Nazaire, a huge church in the middle of the city. A group of Crusaders maniacally bolted the doors from the outside and put the building to the torch. The screams of those inside were bloodcurdling. As many as 6,000 people were burned to death inside the church. Completely engulfed in flames, the cathedral collapsed with a concussive roar.

Andre arrived at the Lion Rouge and called to a fleeing couple.

"Which is the house of Iolande?"

They pointed to her home. As Guillaume was unable to hear any of the words Andre was saying, his curiosity remained at the highest peak. He watched as Andre entered Iolande's house.

Once inside, Andre looked around and called out the names of Simon and Arianne. They both emerged from the cellar.

Arianne shouted with glee, "Andre!"

"Thank God you're safe! Where is Roland?"

Simon answered, "He has gone to the Rue Droite to get my sister!"

Arianne added, "It is the house next to the blacksmith's!"

Andre informed them of the escape routes that had been designated by the allies of the Cathars so they might all rendezvous after the carnage had abetted.

"The fighting is moving in this direction. Make your way quickly to the Rue de la Tour. There are crypts near the northern end; hide in one of them until we come for you. If we are delayed, do not fear. Wait until nightfall and slip out through the gate. There will be few troops in that sector. Go to the house of Vergiers and we will meet you there. You will be safe. I go now to find Roland and your sister."

After he left, Arianne and Simon fled through the streets in an effort to reach the crypts. If they were able to get there, they hoped they would find safety and perhaps meet up with some other Cathars.

As Arianne glanced back, she caught sight of Guillaume. He saw her as well and spurred his horse in pursuit. Arianne pulled Simon into an alley.

Unfortunately, the alley emerged into a very large and open grassy area. Realizing their vulnerability, they ran toward a cluster of houses. But Guillaume intercepted them before they could reach the safety of concealment. Simon pushed Arianne behind him to protect her.

The Templar commander sneered.

"Well, well!"

Simon proclaimed boldly, "So the wolf descends upon the fold at last!"

"I see no sheep here. Only heretics!"

Arianne stepped out from behind Simon and faced Guillaume, standing shoulder to shoulder with her father. She spoke up.

"Now you will see how the righteous die!"

Guillaume dismounted and drew his sword.

Simon spoke with pride, "You may kill our bodies, but you have no power over our souls."

"The Holy Father condemns you to Hell!"

"You cannot frighten us with your myth of endless punishment."

Guillaume looked menacingly at Arianne then spotted Aisha's Arabic talisman around her neck.

"What have you there? An Infidel charm?"

He clutched the talisman and she answered, "A gift, from a true man!"

"From a traitor to God and country, more like it—if he keeps company with heathen Saracens! Or maybe you play the whore to Saracens?"

Arianne attempted to slap him, but he grabbed her hand and twisted it. Simon tried to free her. Guillaume delivered a swift kick to his stomach which knocked him to the ground, gasping for breath.

In the heat of anger, Arianne defiantly blurted out an unexpected piece of information.

"He is no traitor, but a free and honorable man—a man you have wronged!"

Guillaume was suddenly interested.

"A man I have wronged?"

"My husband—yes, my husband—Roland de Provence! I die proudly with his name on my lips!"

Guillaume was momentarily stunned at hearing this. Then his anger boiled over. With a roar of frustration and outrage, he slapped Arianne and she stumbled from the blow.

Simon rose to protect her, pointing Roland's sword and seeking an opening in Guillaume's defenses. Guillaume ran him through. Simon collapsed, grievously wounded and bleeding profusely. Arianne rushed to him.

"My child. Keep your courage and resist these bigots. You may forgive them in your heart, but fight them with your body. I go now to join your mother."

Arianne sobbed, "Father, know that I carry Roland's child—your grandchild—within my womb."

As Simon died, he looked into her eyes, "This is a blessing."

CHAPTER 64

Down a narrow street not far away, Andre encountered Roland and Iolande running toward him.

Andre shouted above the din, "Simon and Arianne have gone to the crypts along the Rue de la Tour. If we are separated, we will meet at the house of Vergiers. Take my horse and sword."

Roland mounted the horse but refused the weapon.

"You'll need your sword to protect Iolande."

Roland rode off, unarmed, toward the crypts.

Along the way, he spotted a group of bowmen climbing up to take a position on a rooftop. Roland called out to them.

"I am Roland, the son of your ally, the Comte de Provence. I need a bow."

"We have naught to spare."

"I implore you! Help me take a few of these devils to my grave with me!"

One of the archers acquiesced and handed him first a longbow, then a quiver of arrows.

Roland thanked him and rode off through a maze of winding streets. He eventually emerged onto the farthest end of the open grassy area, when he saw Guillaume in the distance threatening Arianne. Guillaume's sword was raised and Roland could see he was about to strike.

Roland was at a distance of over 200 yards. He realized there was no time to approach any closer. He quickly dismounted and notched an arrow. This was clearly an impossible distance to shoot with a bow, but Roland focused on his target. The sounds of battle faded far into the background of his consciousness as he entered the silence of his meditative state. He took aim, then closed his eyes and breathed slowly and deeply. So far removed from the chaos around him, he could hear the sound of his own heartbeat. He opened his eyes and adjusted the angle of his body slightly by moving his feet. He completely identified himself with his target.

At the same moment, Guillaume screamed in fury at Arianne, his rage fueled by the bloodlust around him, his anger at his own attraction to her, and his perverse sexual jealousy that Roland had had this woman.

"Traitor! Heretic! Whore!"

He was about to strike her—to cut her down—as she courageously attempted to stand, her simple dress stained with her father's blood.

Roland released his arrow. Its long flight was like that of a hawk in the perfection of its trajectory. As Guillaume's muscles tensed to deliver the fatal blow, Roland's arrow slammed into him. Guillaume's eyes widened in surprise and terror. The sword fell from his hand as he collapsed to the ground.

Roland leapt back on his horse and rode furiously to his wife. When he dismounted he saw that Simon was lying dead. He embraced Arianne with a mixture of relief and sorrow.

Just then Andre and Iolande came around the corner into the field. Iolande flung herself onto her brother's body and shrieked in despair. Roland looked at Andre. They exchanged battle-weary looks.

Andre looked at Guillaume's fallen body.

"It appears now that I am commander, though it gives me little satisfaction. Simon was a man of honor."

As he looked on at this scene of tragedy and carnage, Andre spoke again.

"Come quickly! Take the horses. We must leave the city. We will gather at the house of retreat. Death must await another day."

CHAPTER 65

They arrived at the house of Vergiers on the hillside overlooking Béziers. Some others were already there. As the light fell through the late afternoon, more survivors continued to arrive.

By early evening, the fighting had been over for some time. Fires still burned in the city while horse carts carried away the dead. The few who lived and could walk wandered around in shock, surveying the horror and searching for any other survivors.

Wounded citizens fortunate enough to find the safe house were being treated by various Cathar healers. An exhausted Arianne was among those ministering to people in need. She looked vacant, spent, half alive.

Later that night Roland, Arianne, Iolande, Andre, some Cathars, and a few Templar brothers were sitting on the floor.

Roland said wearily, "A French city has been devastated by Frenchmen. If there is any victory here, it is the triumph of ignorance, superstition, and intolerance."

Iolande was distressed by her understanding of the doctrinal errors of the Cathars that she had learned and taught to others her entire life.

"We Cathars must confront our own ignorance. How many of us surrendered to our deaths like sheep to the slaughter? God imbued us with a will to survive. Is the fruit of our faith to be capitulation to evil? My brother, at least, awakened sufficiently to try to protect Arianne today. We need to examine ourselves if we intend to survive."

Arianne answered her, "Sometimes we need the darkness to see the Light."

Roland continued, "We must learn to think for ourselves. It

is the task of every one of us to discover how best to live. We have all been forced to abandon the beliefs and teachings we once held dear.

"Each of us has rejected the false beliefs of Rome. By marrying Arianne, I abandoned my Templar vow of chastity. Andre renounced his vow of obedience by working secretly against Guillaume. Arianne defied her status as a Parfait by embracing me. Simon blessed our union and thus betrayed an important tenet of his faith—then died like a warrior with a sword in his hand.

"We are called 'heretics' because we love God more than the rigid forms and dogmas by which we have been taught to worship Him. We have all been compelled to discard the worn-out creeds of our past."

Andre spoke for the first time, "And tomorrow?"

"Andre, it is now your destiny to lead our Templar brethren in their quest for Truth. With Guillaume's death, his suspicion against you has also died. You will be able to work more freely.

"Arianne and I must leave these parts. We're a danger to all of you. We will head north in the morning. Iolande, you may, of course, join us in our journeys."

She replied kindly, "Thank you, Roland. But with my brother dead, my place is here with our people. More suffering lies ahead. There will be many opportunities to serve."

Arianne took Roland's hand and laid her head on his shoulder.

Andre spoke again, "Is this then the end of our mission together?"

Roland reflected on the day of his leave-taking from Al-Kaph.

"I can only repeat the words of Sinan. Whenever we work to lengthen the Chain of Light, we're drawn closer together. This is not the end of our mission. It is the beginning."

"Where will it lead?"

"To a new era! Liberty stirs in the womb of Time. I feel it."

A vision rose before him and he seemed to channel its message to the others.

"It is the absolute right of every individual to live without interference. Men and women will ever rise to fight tyranny and oppression, and they will win. Old institutions and worn-out ideas will fall. Dogmas and superstitions will wither and die. All people will one day live in the Light—confident, free, and without fear!"

They sat in silence, pondering the import of these words.

Roland rose and walked outside to look upon the stars. After some precious moments of solitude and reflection, he turned to re-enter the house. As he did so, he caught sight of a glowing green bird sitting on a nearby tree branch. He approached and bowed his head, then looked up. They held each other's gaze in silent communion until the bird flew off into the night.

The next morning at dawn, Roland saddled two horses. Arianne joined him. Iolande and Andre brought bundles of food for the couple's journey. As the sun rose higher, Roland and Arianne mounted their horses.

Andre looked up at his friend and mentor.

"Go forward in joy and victory, Roland. May God and his angels keep you safe."

Roland grasped his hand.

"My dearest friend, Andre. As Sinan once told me, 'Angels bend down their wings to a seeker of knowledge.'"

Arianne leaned down and kissed Iolande.

Then she and Roland rode off, side by side. They extended their arms and their hands touched briefly.

Roland noticed a single rose, which had climbed over the top of an old stone wall that bordered a portion of the road. He remembered Aisha's words in the courtyard of Al-Kaph on that fateful day of his departure.

"The rose is a symbol of the unfolding of the soul."

He caught Arianne's eye as he rode over to the wall to pick the flower. He rejoined his beloved and handed her the rose.

Finis

AFTERWORD

The mass arrests of the Knights Templar in France on Friday the 13th, 1307 began a seven-year ordeal. Countless hundreds of innocent men were rounded up and imprisoned throughout Catholic Europe. Many were subjected to unspeakable tortures; many were burnt alive at the stake; all were subject to a campaign of vilification and slander the likes of which had rarely been seen before. The collusion between the French king and his puppet pope gave birth to the technique of the Big Lie—tortuously constructed by manipulative publicists who sought to turn contemporary cultural heroes into objects of scorn and hatred. The real crime of the Templars was threefold: They were so strongly identified with the Crusades that when Europe was ignominiously defeated in 1292, they were widely blamed; they retained great wealth built during their successful efforts to financially support a two hundred-year military campaign; and, as the pope's private army, they had developed an intolerable independence from the changing power structure of feudal Europe.

Half a century before the destruction of the Templars, the massed hordes of the late Genghiz Khan's Mongolian army—under the leadership of his grandson—tore through the Caucasus mountain regions of Persia in 1256. They devastated the Assassin power base at Alamut, then systematically extended their conquest to the remaining Assassin fortresses, massacring and pillaging as they went. The Assassins lost the political autonomy they had carved out 166 years earlier. Some Nizaris were able to survive by concealing themselves among the Iranian Sufi orders of the day. One well-known example was Shams-i-Tabriz, the spiritual master of the poet Jalal-al-Din Rumi, founder of the Mevlevi Sufi order of Whirling Dervishes.

Half a century before the campaign against the Assassins, the launch of the Albigensian Crusades in 1209 by the Roman Catholic Church was responsible for the death of thousands of men, women, and children over the next twenty years. The Albigensian Crusades marked the beginning of the Inquisition that terrorized Europe for hundreds of years thereafter, and to which the Templars also fell victim.

It is to honor the memory of these spiritual heroes that this story was written. And especially to hymn the Invisible Reality that I believe motivated some of the most aware among them.

HISTORICAL LIBERTIES

Literary license has been taken with the timeline of the main events described in this story. Otherwise, the historical details presented here are accurate. The characters are either historical persons or fictional creations and the author assumes the reader can be trusted to judge which is which.

The highly detailed main action of the novel extends from a Crusader mission to Syria in 1204 to the first battle (i.e., massacre) of the Albigensian Crusades in 1209. This is a compressed chronology by a decade.

The visit of Henry II, count of Champagne and king of Jerusalem, to the Assassin headquarters actually took place in 1194. We do not know the specific castle he visited, nor the name of the Old Man of the Mountain who so startled him by signaling the death leap of his fidais. Conrad of Montferrat, the previous king of Jerusalem, was assassinated in 1192. Richard the Lionhearted's peace treaty with Saladin was concluded in 1192, after which he left the Holy Land to begin his return to Europe. Saladin died in 1193.

Rashid al-Din Sinan also died in 1193. He was a childhood friend and virtually the same age as Hasan II, rather than his young disciple as in this story. Sinan was a far less stationary leader than depicted here. He traveled continually from castle to castle in the Nusayri Mountains, maintaining his security and keeping a watchful eye on his network. Despite the frequent references to meals in this tale, it is said that Sinan was never seen to eat or drink. His mystic wisdom, esoteric knowledge, political skill, and impeccable courtesy are all as portrayed in the historical literature, as is his legendary communication with the spirit of Hasan II in the form of the glowing green bird.

One is obligated to mention that historians have suggested two scriptural sources for the learned abbot Arnaud Amaury's appalling statement, "Kill them all, God will know his own." If he actually said it, he may have been paraphrasing Saint Paul, "The Lord knoweth them that are his" [2 Timothy 2:19]. Paul was alluding to Moses in a tense confrontation with rebels, "Even tomorrow the Lord will show who are his, and who is holy; and will cause him to come near unto him: even him whom he hath chosen will he cause to come near unto him" [Numbers 16:5].

A PERSONAL NOTE

I first wrote about the Templars and the Assassins in 1983 in an essay published in *The Equinox* III:10 by the O.T.O. in 1986. That short account combined facts and romance, and echoed the endless fascination of this myth to esotericists since the Middle Ages. In 2001, *The Templars and the Assassins* was published by Inner Traditions. It is a disciplined and carefully sourced account, scrupulously distinguishing between verifiable history and speculation. The text of that book was adapted in 2006 for *An Illustrated History of the Knights Templar*, whose rich collection of historical color images visually conveys the intensity and iconography of the Order. These books have all been well received and I am grateful they continue to prove valuable to so many readers.

In mid-October of 2006, I was approached by movie producer Harvey Rochman, who suggested I write a screenplay based on *The Templars and the Assassins*. I was just finishing up a talk for Mark Stavish that would be delivered in early November at the Masonic Reading Society—a branch of the Institute for Hermetic Studies in Wilkes-Barre, Pennsylvania. I sent the manuscript of the talk to Harvey. He loved the summary of my ideas and encouraged me to write a fictional movie treatment, including a love interest.

Harvey thus reopened the romance and legends of the Templars that had so inflamed me as a young seeker. He gave me permission to once again identify, imagine, and incorporate my own life experience into the story.

Thanksgiving dinner brought Keith Stump to our table. He is well schooled in the Mystery Traditions and an experienced screenwriter. He had spent time in the Middle East as a religious scholar and documentarian. We shared some excellent conversation that day and decided to write the screenplay together. A creative fugue lasted from December 2006 to September 2007.

The screenplay of *Divine Warriors* was the result. Harvey and I spent the next eight years attempting to get it produced—with several seemingly very bright rays of hope illuminating our path.

Ultimately, I accepted the fact that I had gone about the process in reverse order. A novel would add meat to the bones of the story and allow me the freedom to work in the medium I know best. Thanksgiving of 2015 found my wife Nancy, daughter Rachel, and myself at the home of our friends Dan and Gwen Gunther. Here I began the work of transforming the already much-rewritten screenplay into a novel. This book adds over 50 percent more material.

The photo on page 18, and shown again here opposite, is an eight-hundred-year-old silver coin minted at Alamut. It was a gift from my dear friend, numismatist David Vagi. This ancient talisman is believed to have been a "donative," a gift from the Imam, because it bears no date or mint mark. It was struck during the reign of Muhammad III (r. 1221–1255), also known as Ala al-Din or Aladdin. Amir Modak describes it as a "passport to heaven" given by the Imam to his favored recipient.

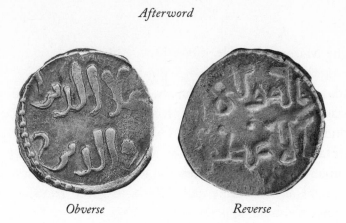

Obverse *Reverse*

The inscription on the obverse reads, *Alā al-Dīn wa al-Dunyā*, meaning "Exalted [One] of the Faith and the World." The reverse reads, *Al-Mawlana al-'A'zam* meaning "The Greatest Lord." (With thanks to William Hamblin.) It weighs 1.85 grams and measures 14mm.

The millennium-old story of the Templars and Assassins was never written by a participant. This novel may then fill an important gap and be the most accurate of my efforts. Why? Because here, so many of the events described match my own life experience as an initiate on the same Path as that of its characters.

Is this the way it "really happened"? Who knows?

What I can say is this is the way it really happened for me.

In hopes it resonates with the reader.

ACKNOWLEDGMENTS

Keith Stump, co-writer of the screenplay from which this novel was derived, deserves pride of place in my thanks. The process of creative development we shared was as mysterious and inspiring as it is indescribable.

Harvey Rochman opened the door to this entire epic with an e-mail and a phone call. His inspiration, friendship, and guidance are much appreciated.

Nancy Wasserman earns the Head of the Class award for patience and support. Her important creative contributions to the story are significant. She reviewed countless iterations of the screenplay and novel. Her practical advice was essential during the many twists and turns of this process, during which she maintained a constant faith in its value.

Lisa Wagner and Stella Grey made invaluable editorial suggestions. Their brilliance has improved my efforts by many orders of magnitude. My lifetime friend Claire Deem's kindness in reviewing the manuscript—and her insights, suggestions, and encouragement—are much appreciated.

Bill Corsa, Kittie Palakovich, and Michael Antinori guided me through the contractual labyrinth that allowed this book to emerge from the chaos of its beginning. All three made important creative contributions that greatly enhanced the story.

Donald Weiser and Yvonne Paglia, Dan and Gwen Gunther, Tom and Rebekah Schaefer, Richard Capuro, Peter Levenda, Rafael Aguilar, Kent Finne, Genevieve Breeze, Karen Lindenberger, Lindy Wisdom, Emma Silecchia, Michael Patterson, and Michael Elgert offered support, discussion, and friendship throughout. Wileda Wasserman believed in this novel long before it was even conceived.

Jon Graham, Ehud Sperling, and Jeanie Levitan will always retain my love, trust, appreciation, and respect. Thanks to Mindy Branstetter for her intelligence and professionalism.

Mark Stavish's invitation to speak at the Masonic Reading Society in 2006 challenged me to summarize my thoughts on the contact between the Assassins, Cathars, and Templars in a brief and concise form. Father David Novak helped make my comments on the early history of Christianity more accurate.

David Vagi's birthday gift of the Assassin coin in 2008 humbled and inspired me more than I can ever say. We had searched for it for ten years. Master jeweler Brian Cundiff set it in a ring on a bed of cotton beneath a diver's crystal, protecting and preserving it for future generations.

Randy Cain and Irv Lehman taught me the technique of natural point of aim as used by Roland and Aisha. Arlene Stimmel introduced me to Richard Bates, an archery expert, who helped me to adapt it to archery.

My late and dear friend Jim Garvey and I shared our enthusiasm for the term "Divine Warriors" for so long I'm not sure which one of us used it first.

Amir Modak, Leah Einwalter, Daniel and Julia Pineda, Illia Tulloch, Jesse Cook, Shelley Marmor, Patricio Bravo, and Ben Wilder provided much assistance with the screenplay of *Divine Warriors* and potential film production.

Thanks to Emily Elizabeth, who introduced me to her father, Keith. I also appreciate the support I received during the screenplay stage from George and Julie Kalivretenos, Priscilla Costello, Bernard Friedrich, Jerry and Doris Caplan, Ed Asner, Kevin Greene, Roger and Martina Danchik, Joey Reynolds, Bob Coen, Sean Stone, John Marks, John Wesley Chisolm, Gonzalo Escudero, Heather Eisenstadt and Alan Rock, Peter Adam, Phil Nutman, Suzanne Kovacs, Sinta Weisz, Eleanor Jackson-Peel, Heidi Bordogna, Marta Garcia, Lucas Daré, John Milius, Norman Steinberg, Brenda Kovrig, and Poke Runyan.